"You think I'm an idiot, don't you?"

"*No*, I don't," Von replied. "But I am starting to question your mental state."

"I'm perfectly sane. Which is surprising considering I've been harassed all afternoon. Do you see this?" Dani screeched, holding up her phone. "Call after call from anonymous numbers. It's interesting that this started right after our confrontation at Cole's. You expect me to believe you know nothing about it?"

"Yes. That's exactly what I'm expecting. It's the truth. I'm sorry this is happening to you. But believe me, I have nothing to do with it."

"I'm sorry, but I'm not convinced. If it isn't you, it's probably someone from your company who can't get past the bad blood between us."

"All right, prove it. Show me evidence that backs your claims. You're grasping at straws. You obviously have no leads. So you're taking the easy route, and blaming your shortcomings on my company."

"I may not have the evidence yet, but it's just a matter of time. I'll figure it out. I always do."

FEARLESS PURSUIT

DENISE N. WHEATLEY

To my parents, Ronald and Donna

Recycling programs for this product may not exist in your area.

ISBN-13: 978-1-335-69047-0

Fearless Pursuit

For questions and comments about the quality of this book, please contact us at CustomerService@Harlequin.com.

Harlequin Enterprises ULC
22 Adelaide St. West, 41st Floor
Toronto, Ontario M5H 4E3, Canada
www.Harlequin.com

HarperCollins Publishers
Macken House, 39/40 Mayor Street Uppe
Dublin 1, D01 C9W8, Ireland
www.HarperCollins.com

Printed in Lithuania

Denise N. Wheatley loves happy endings and the art of storytelling. Her novels run the romance gamut, and she strives to pen entertaining books that embody matters of the heart. She's an RWA member and holds a BA in English from the University of Illinois. When Denise isn't writing, she enjoys watching true crime TV and chatting with readers. Follow her on social media.

Instagram: @Denise_Wheatley_Writer
X: @DeniseWheatley
BookBub: @DeniseNWheatley
Goodreads: Denise N. Wheatley

Books by Denise N. Wheatley

Harlequin Intrigue

A West Coast Crime Story

The Heart-Shaped Murders
Danger in the Nevada Desert
Homicide at Vincent Vineyard
Hometown Homicide
Preyed Upon
Fearless Pursuit

An Unsolved Mystery Book

Cold Case True Crime

Bayou Christmas Disappearance
Backcountry Cover-Up

Harlequin Medical Romance

ER Doc's Las Vegas Reunion

Visit the Author Profile page at Harlequin.com.

CAST OF CHARACTERS

Danielle (Dani) Miller—Maxwell, Arizona's chief of police

Von Reed—Owner of Reed Protective Services (RPS), and Dani's rival

Troy Miller—Dani's brother, who works for the Maxwell PD

Chloe Grant—Dani's best friend and a true crime podcaster who consults with the Maxwell PD

Kevin Freelain—Vice President of Reed Protective Services and Von's right-hand man

Gene Miller—Dani's father and Maxwell's former chief of police

Hamilton Reed—Von's father and the retired owner of Reed Protective Services

Chapter One

"Chief Miller! Would you mind taking a picture with me and my girls?"

Dani cringed at the request. She still hadn't gotten used to all the attention she'd gained after capturing the first serial killer to prey on Maxwell, Arizona, nearly a year ago.

"Pleeease!" the young woman begged in response to Dani's silence.

The chief tugged awkwardly at her black moto jacket, resisting the urge to dash out the door of the Zonian Bar & Grill.

"Of course," she finally said, relenting at the woman's hopeful dimpled grin. "Where should I stand?"

"Yesss! Right here in the middle of us!"

As Dani took her place in the center of the group, the crowd around them burst into cheers. The chief's face burned with embarrassment. She dismissed the applause with a wave, fixating on the woman's satin Bride to Be sash to avoid all the gawking.

The women around her adjusted their teal bridesmaid-style dresses, then kicked their cowboy boots high in the air. "Our girl's getting *marrieeed*!" one of them squealed. Peace signs and heart hands hovered over their heads like crowns while a fellow patron snapped photos.

Dani stood stiff as a statue, barely breathing while struggling not to squint at the camera's bright flash. Those flames of self-consciousness traveled down to her neck when she noticed her former classmates looking on. Their prying eyes felt more like glaring spotlights as they observed the awe-struck exchange.

They'd gathered at the bar to celebrate their twenty-year class reunion. The Zonian was owned by their former senior class president, so after a weekend filled with cookouts, softball in the park and snowboarding at Cole's Ski Resort, it was only right that they end the festivities there. Dani just wished she could've celebrated privately like the rest of her peers rather than be singled out by eager admirers.

"Thank you so much, *Daniii*!" the bride-to-be sang out before slapping her hand over her mouth. "Oops, I—I'm so sorry, Danielle. I mean, Chief Miller. Congrats on being the queen of Maxwell!"

Dani's bemused head nod was punctuated with a chuckle. "The queen of Maxwell? That's a bit of a stretch, but you're welcome. And congratulations to you on your upcoming nuptials."

The chief's voice faded into the beer-scented air as the woman raised her drink, sending tequila dribbling down her arm. "Thanks, girl!" she exclaimed before twirling off to the pulsating rhythm of a hip-hop beat blaring through the speakers.

Just when Dani turned to rejoin her group, she noticed a set of dark, piercing eyes watching her intently.

"Ugh," she groaned, unable to swallow her disgust. The sight of Von Reed had that effect on her. Most women had the opposite reaction. They gravitated toward his smooth reddish-brown skin that deepened during the summer months and strong features that softened when he smiled. Even Dani couldn't deny that he had the whole tall, dark and handsome thing going on. Problem was, he knew it. And while others saw him as charismatic and confident, Dani found him annoying and arrogant.

"Why are you even here..." she mumbled to herself.

But Von had every right to be there considering he, too, was a former classmate. Regardless of that fact, his presence was unnerving. He and Dani's contentious history ran deep. Generationally deep. What had been ignited by their fathers was further fueled by the two of them. And Dani had no interest in snuffing out the rivalry.

"Hey," her best friend, Chloe, whispered in her ear. "Have you noticed how Von's been watching you all night?"

"Of course I have," Dani responded with a slight eye roll. "How could I not?"

Close since childhood, Chloe had witnessed the contention between Dani and Von worsen over time. She'd missed a fair share of it after relocating to Chicago in her early twenties, becoming a big-city detective and losing herself in a toxic relationship. The move sent their friendship into a tailspin as it ruined plans to take over the Maxwell PD. They'd managed to reconcile, however, when Chloe returned home last October and began dating Dani's brother, Officer Troy Miller.

"Look at him," Chloe muttered, nodding in Von's direction. "Clearly he sees us watching him. Yet he's just standing here, shamelessly staring you down."

DANI'S HEAD WHIPPED BACK toward the desert-themed bar's succulent mural wall. It wasn't hard to miss Von's brooding six-foot-three presence, looming in front of a bright green prickly pear cactus. He stood with an air of cockiness, his thick hands tucked casually into his jeans as if he were posing for a magazine shoot. His penetrating gaze was like a freshly lit match, igniting a spark of annoyance in her gut. It sent Dani spinning around, mad that she'd even acknowledged his presence.

"I wonder if Von's company is working security for tonight's event," Chloe said, craning her neck while pulling her long, straight bob behind her ears.

Shifting her eyes discreetly, Dani searched his broad chest for the Reed Protective Services' cream-and-navy shield. Von had been running his family's firm, better known as RPS, since his father's recent retirement. Tonight, his pale blue button-down was logo-free. "It looks like he's off duty. So I guess the only work he's putting in is studying every move I make. And of course his goofy sidekick is right there with him," Dani added, referring to RPS's vice president, Kevin Freelain.

"Oh, but of course. I do hate that Von is so handsome considering he's off-limits. I actually think you two would be good together. If you think about it, you two have a lot in common. Plus he's got those dark, deep-set eyes, that bright, mischievous smile—"

"Um, I'm sorry," Dani interrupted with a flick of her wrist. "But have you lost your mind? We do not give compliments to the enemy. Plus I don't have a thing in common with that man. Now you'd better quit while you're ahead before I tell my brother you've got a crush on Von."

"Now *that* would be a bold-faced lie," Chloe shot back before signaling the bartender and ordered another round of merlot. "Listen, it's Sunday. The last night of our reunion weekend. Let's not ruin it with all this talk of Von. Instead, we'll have another drink and toast to the fact that you actually showed up this weekend."

"Wait, what is that supposed to mean?"

"Please don't get defensive. It's a compliment. I'm proud of you for opening yourself up to a social life after cracking the biggest case of your career. So here's to more outings, more peopling, and dare I say it, you meeting the love of your life."

"Whoa, whoa, slow down, sis. I appreciate the intentions, but let's not go too far. Nevertheless, cheers."

Just as the pair clinked glasses, Troy approached, his tall, lean physique moving effortlessly through the crowded bar. "Wait, what are we toasting to? The fact that Dani is winning the stare-down between her and Von? Or that Maxwell PD's presence is so heavy tonight that we've managed to outnumber RPS's crew?"

"C," Dani rebutted. "None of the above. Von may be acting foolish, but I am in no way participating in a stare-down. And as for Maxwell PD, there is no competition. Contrary to what RPS may believe, they have zero authority in this town."

"True. But I can understand why they think they do, though."

"And why is that?"

Troy held up his hand, ticking off points on his fingers one by one. "For starters, some of the townspeople do have a tendency to call them over us when crimes are committed."

Through narrowed eyes, Dani glared at Troy, her sharp expression icy enough to turn the warm bar cold. The reaction silenced him. As Troy retreated against a stool, Chloe's knowing glance stated the obvious. Certain topics were touchy. The rivalry between the Maxwell PD and RPS was one of them. More specifically, the beef between the Miller and Reed families.

It all started when Dani's and Von's fathers entered the Maxwell PD's police academy together. Gene Miller and Hamilton Reed grew close during their journey to becoming officers. They'd remained tight up until the point where Gene was named police chief. It was a position that Hamilton had long vied for. He'd tried his best to get over the snub, despite being convinced he was the better man for the job.

Once Gene became boss, Hamilton felt as though he was too hard on him and overly critical of his job performance. Hamilton was convinced the reprimands would tarnish his record and block future job promotions. So he quit, cracked open his savings and established RPS.

For Hamilton, launching the company hadn't been easy. He'd never dreamed of owning a security firm. His goal had always been to work for the police department. But his confidence in the company grew when several officers quit the force and joined his team, which was a no-brainer after he offered a higher salary and flexible schedules.

The upside was that RPS became Maxwell's premiere protection service, providing security for the most prestigious businesses, events and private citizens. Yet the downside ran deeper than Hamilton's rivalry with Gene. Tensions between the men divided law enforcement officers throughout the town.

Chaos erupted when the townspeople became split over who to call when crimes occurred. Some reached out to the police department, but the number of officers had decreased due to the exodus. The force was stretched thin. Complaints began pouring in, accusing Maxwell PD of slow responses to crime scenes. As a result, some residents turned to RPS, knowing the officers were former law enforcement and familiar with the community.

"Hellooo," Chloe said, snapping her fingers in front of Dani's face. "What's wrong? Did the wine just hypnotize you?"

"No, sorry… I was just thinking about this never-ending feud."

"I can't believe it's still going on. Especially now that both of your fathers have retired."

"Yeah, well, it seems to have gotten worse since I was named police chief and Von started running RPS."

"I can attest to that," Troy interjected, gently tugging at his goatee. "Dani went through hell after being promoted. Like our dad, she lost several officers to RPS after becoming chief due to their jealousy, resentment, all of that…"

"Yeah," Chloe said, nodding so furiously that her hair swept across her face. "RPS's security team was asserting their authority all over town, acting like they possessed the same amount of power as the force."

"Exactly," Dani agreed. "That's why Von and I have had so many unresolved confrontations that only made things worse between us."

She took a long sip of wine and swallowed hard, the burn in her throat matching the irritation in her head. Flashbacks to where it all started flipped through her mind like pages from her diary. The way they'd grown up together, attending the same schools and traveling in the same circles. Yet it was understood that there was to be no socializing between the Reed and Miller families.

That unwritten rule prompted Dani to keep her distance, which wasn't difficult considering she and Von were complete opposites. While he was busy being an attention-seeking athlete and party-hopping playboy, she was focused on her studies and rolled with a select clique of friends.

"And just like that," Chloe said, "he's gone."

"Who's gone?" Dani asked.

"Von. He's like the Black Panther. In and out before anyone notices."

"Don't compare that man to my favorite superhero. And I'm glad he's gone. I was getting sick of him staring over here all night. Anyway, speaking of leaving…" Dani glanced down at the time on her phone. "I need to get going. I've got an early morning. Budget meeting prep."

Troy slid his empty beer bottle onto the bar and threw an arm around Dani. "Before you even say it, I'm right behind you, Chief. Since I'm vying for that promotion to detective, I already know that getting to work early is a good look. You ready, Chloe?"

"I am. I've got an early day, too. The latest recording of *Preyed Upon* isn't gonna edit itself."

"Ooh," Dani breathed before waving goodbye to a group of classmates, then heading toward the exit. "I've been waiting for the next podcast episode to air. What's this one about?"

"A wealthy businessman in Atlanta who's also a major womanizer. He was known for dating several ladies at once, and eventually, that lifestyle caught up to him. One of his many companions ended up killing him."

Troy pulled open the door, the moonlight flickering across his gaping eyes. "*Damn.* I think I heard about that guy. Didn't the killer beat him over the head with an alarm clock or something along those lines?"

"Yes, she did. And her DNA was found all over his bedroom. But since her profile hadn't been entered into the national database, the suspect was able to elude law enforcement for almost a decade. During that time, she murdered a couple of her other lovers, too."

Dani clutched her black snakeskin purse, wincing at the lurid details. "That is just awful. I'm glad they were finally able to apprehend her, otherwise more people would have had their lives destroyed."

"True," Troy chimed in. He stopped in front of a faux Joshua tree, its twinkling lights rivaling the stars scattered across the sky. "Where'd you park, D?"

"Right around the corner. By the time I got here, the lot was full and every space on the block was taken."

"Well, we're in the lot, but we'll walk you to your car. Lead the way."

"Please," Dani scoffed, swinging her bag in the air. "You don't have to do that. I'll be fine. I've got my bestie on me."

"So you've traded me in for a Glock 22?" Chloe quipped.

"Absolutely not. You and I are beyond best friends. We're

more like sisters. I'm just waiting on *somebody* to make that official."

When Chloe wiggled her fingerless left hand in front of Troy, he grabbed her by the waist and pulled her close. "Patience, my love. And on that note, Dani, have a good night. See you in the morning."

"See you mañana."

"And hey!" Troy called out. "The day we decide to make things official is coming sooner rather than later. So don't you worry."

"Trust me, I'm not. You know better than to let a good woman get away!"

Their laughter floated through the night air, drifting into the distance as the threesome went their separate ways. Dani set off down the block, the darkness deepening with each step.

Mountain peaks loomed majestically in the distance as faint moonbeams illuminated their foreboding presence. Most establishments had already closed. Their pitch-black windows reflected the eerie silence blanketing the street, which had been alive with shoppers, diners and moviegoers just a few hours ago. The vibes now felt oddly still, with only the occasional flicker of headlights breaking the monotony.

Dani reached the corner and made an abrupt left turn. A sharp crack in the asphalt trapped her boot's heel, threatening to send her plummeting down the steep incline. She grabbed hold of the white stucco wall beside her, the rough surface scraping her nails as she steadied herself.

"Please do not roll your damn ankle," Dani uttered, blaming the misstep on lack of streetlights.

She activated her cell phone's flashlight, then tiptoed to her vehicle, aiming the beam toward the uneven pavement. Stopping in front of her burgundy Jeep, Dani leaned against the hood while digging through her purse for the key fob. It wasn't there. She patted down the pockets of her boyfriend jeans. Not there, either.

Did I lock it inside the car?

An out-of-towner would've been frightened by the stillness surrounding her. But Dani was used to it. Sunday nights on the main thoroughfare were relatively dead. Yet tonight, something about the silence seemed out of place. The desolation hit harder than usual.

Life in Maxwell was once safe and secure, to the point where residents left their doors unlocked and walked their dogs in the middle of the night. But ever since a serial killer descended upon their town last year, the community was on high alert. It didn't matter that the offender had been convicted and would spend the rest of his life in prison. Maxwell had been tainted, and there was no going back. The townspeople no longer felt protected beneath a comforting veil of security. They weren't an exception to the worst criminal acts. At this point, anything could happen.

The memory of all they'd endured sent a chill through Dani that could rival a subzero sweep. She tightened the belt on her jacket, then continued the search for her fob until it hit her palm.

Dani tapped the unlock button. Waited for the headlights to blink. They didn't.

"What in the hell..."

A vehicle parked farther down the block lit up. Dani took a closer look at the license plate. A pang of foolishness almost knocked her to the ground. She was standing at the wrong Jeep.

At least nobody saw that, she thought, laughing at herself before continuing down the street.

Dani could only see a few feet ahead thanks to her dying cell phone's fading light. That unsettling chill returned as she shuffled down the narrowing road. It resurrected thoughts of the bad omen still clinging to the town. Pushing the frightening thoughts aside, Dani quickened her pace, her heels clicking against the asphalt as she broke into a near jog.

A wave of relief rolled through her when she finally approached her vehicle. Dani's jagged breathing steadied once she climbed inside and slammed the door shut. She swiftly started the engine, then repositioned the rearview mirror.

Darkness covered the rear windshield. As her eyes adjusted, a shape emerged, silently rising from the back seat.

What the...

Dani grabbed the door handle, her heart thrashing against her rib cage, then fluttering uncontrollably. The rhythmless beat pounded her eardrums. She pressed her body against the door. But before she could exit the vehicle, a cold, sharp wire sliced into her throat.

Her neck hit the headrest. A stream of hot breath singed her eardrum when she was pulled against the back of her seat. Dani gasped, unable to release the scream trapped inside her throat. She slammed her hand against the passenger seat, desperately fumbling for her purse. One jerking motion from the attacker sent her arm flailing. A loud thud confirmed that she'd knocked the clutch to the floor.

Dani's nails sliced into her skin as she clawed at the wire. The assailant yanked harder, sharp steel ripping at her fingertips. Her breathing faltered. Grew thin. Ragged. Dani's surroundings blurred as her eyes rolled into the back of her head. The cord snaked around the back of her neck as cracked leather gloves scratched her flesh.

Just as she felt herself fading, the cord shifted a fraction of an inch. Dani inhaled sharply, oxygen tearing through her lungs like a silent scream. She gripped her throat. Slammed her hand against the door to try to escape. But she could barely move.

Tears of frustration sprang to Dani's eyes. She couldn't get away. Couldn't grab her gun and shoot the attacker dead. Dread burned her chest at the thought of him choking the life out of her, leaving her slumped in the seat. Dead.

Dani's eyes flew open when the wire's deadly grip released, its cold metal slithering away from her throat. The back door popped open. Her attacker fled from the vehicle and shot down the street.

Throwing herself toward the passenger seat, she ripped open her clutch and grabbed her Glock. Dani lunged from the Jeep so violently that she nearly hit the ground. She steadied herself, gasping as brutal pain throbbed inside her throat.

Stay on your feet! Move!

Dani pushed through the agony, her limp jog turning into a frantic sprint as she chased after the heavy footsteps. Their menacing beat echoed like a soundtrack from the past. To a time when Maxwell was under attack. And no one was safe.

The figure, dressed in all black, faded into the darkness. Taking a shot would've been too risky. So Dani held her fire. But the suspect didn't.

Pow!

"Drop your weapon!" she yelled after a bullet ricocheted past her ear.

Pow! Pow!

Dani veered off the sidewalk and ducked down behind a parked car. Peered over the hood. Listened as the fleeing footsteps waned, then disappeared.

Creeping along the side of the car, she drew her weapon and took aim. The street was empty. Just like that, her attacker had vanished as quickly as he'd appeared.

Chapter Two

"Talk to me," Von said, sliding his laptop across the teakwood desk and opening the calendar. "What's on the docket for this week?"

Kevin flipped open his embossed leather notebook and scanned the pages. "Let's see. We've got Grant Ferguson's antique car show happening this weekend, the We Got the Beat Music Festival, Andrea Jordan's wedding—"

"Wait, why does Andrea need security for her wedding?"

"Because she's afraid one of her exes may pop up during the whole *speak now or forever hold your peace* segment of the ceremony and mess everything up."

"Okay then..." Von muttered, typing in the event under Saturday's tab. "What else you got?"

"All of our regular gigs. We'll have officers at the banks, bars and retail stores. Oh, and Five Star Productions will be in town all week filming a movie at Cole's Ski Resort. So we'll need to send out a few extra guys to cover the grounds as well as the set."

"That shouldn't be a problem. Is that it?"

"Yep," Kevin confirmed. "That's it. Unless we get some last-minute calls now that the busy season is kicking off. You know the drill. Tourists hit the town—"

"And all hell inevitably breaks loose," Von injected before gulping down a half cup of lukewarm coffee.

"Don't you think you're being a bit dramatic? It's not *that* bad."

"That's debatable. You can't deny that things are getting worse around here—" Von paused at the ping from his laptop.

A notification popped up, alerting him that the latest edition of *The Maxwell Times* had dropped in his inbox. Von clicked the link. A photo of Dani flashed across the screen. The caption underneath it read, "How Chief Danielle Miller continues to keep Maxwell safe."

"What's wrong?" Kevin asked.

Von quickly relaxed his furrowed brow. "What do you mean?"

"Why are you glaring at your laptop with that scowl on your face?"

"No reason."

He reached for the lid. Before Von could slam it shut, Kevin grabbed the keyboard and swung it around.

"Ohh, no wonder," Kevin said, his frown now rivaling Von's. "Dani made the front page of *The Maxwell Times* again, huh. The last thing that attention-obsessed woman needs is another cover story, praising her for simply doing her job."

"Well…"

"Well what?"

"You do have to give her credit, Kev. This town had never been hit with a crime so brutal. And Dani did manage to solve the case."

"Did she? Or was it her brother and Chloe who cracked it?"

Emitting a condescending chuckle, Von slid the laptop toward the other side of the desk. "Okay, now you're just being cynical. RPS and the Maxwell PD may bump heads from time to time. But we can't take away from the fact that Dani worked the hell out of that investigation. She was under a ton of pressure, too, having just been named chief of police. Not to mention she had the attention of the national news media all over her."

"Hold on, Von. Are my ears deceiving me, or are you actually taking up for your archnemesis?"

"I'd like to think that I'm simply stating facts. Obviously Dani isn't my favorite person in the world. But we have to give credit where credit is due."

"If only your father could hear you now. Hamilton Reed did not build this great company and hand it down to you just for you to turn around and cozy up to your biggest rival—"

"Cozy up?" Von interrupted. "That's a bit of a stretch, isn't it?"

"I don't know. You tell me. Because it's sounding like the secret crush you've had on Dani since high school is rearing its ugly head."

Von snatched his mug and bolted from his chair. "Okay, now you've *completely* lost the script. I think we're done here. Plus I need more coffee."

Responding with a thin-lipped smirk, Kevin followed him out the door. "Whatever, man. Listen, I'll do you a favor and end the interrogation there. But don't forget, I've known you since we were eight. There isn't much you can hide from me."

"Come see me once you get the officers scheduled for those upcoming events," Von shot back over his shoulder while strutting through a maze of cubicles spread across the expansive, loft-style office.

"Way to evade the conversation!"

"I have no idea what you're talking about!"

But that was a lie. He knew exactly what Kevin meant, having spent years trying to hide his attraction to Dani.

As stunning as she'd always been, Dani never flaunted her beauty or intelligence. Von found that extremely appealing. Given the rift between their fathers, however, he couldn't bring himself to cross enemy lines and ask her out. Not that she ever would've agreed. That was made perfectly clear through her standoffish attitude and unbreakable familial bond. Getting anywhere near her was damn near impossible. So Von never tried. Nor had he revealed his true feelings to anyone.

Von knew Dani's disdain toward him stemmed from their fathers' feud. Nevertheless, he'd followed her lead, fronting as if he weren't the least bit interested. But deep down, he always wondered whether she was feeling him, too.

Highly doubtful...

Hovering over the coffee maker inside the break room, Von poured his third cup of the morning. It wasn't like him to down so much caffeine that early. But he needed it to settle his scattered thoughts. It didn't help that Kevin had stormed into his office the moment he'd arrived, throwing his entire routine off course. As the hours ticked by, it felt as though he was running on fumes.

"Von!" the receptionist's shrill voice boomed over the intercom. She still hadn't figured out how to use her inside voice with the new system.

The verbal blow sent a stream of hot coffee dripping down Von's wrist. "Damn it..." he hissed, flinging his burning hand through the air like a spinning windmill. As he set off toward the front of the office, Iga proceeded to make her announcement over the loudspeaker.

"Von, I transferred a call to your office from a Melody Anderson. I repeat, *Melody Anderson.* Since you seem to have stepped away from your desk, she'll be calling your cell phone and asked that you please pick up rather than send her to voicemail like you normally do. Thank you."

Bursts of muffled giggles arose from the cubicles.

"Please get back to work," Von said on the way to his office. The moment he closed to door behind him, his cell rang.

Disregarding Melody's request, he sent her call to voicemail. Von didn't have time to keep explaining to his former fling why he couldn't see her any longer. Plus she knew not to call during peak work hours.

"Von!" Iga's voice roared through the intercom once again. "Sending a call to your office. It's Officer Bryant. He's at Cole's Ski Resort and says it's an emergency!"

Just as he reached for the phone, Kevin stuck his head inside the office. "I don't like the sound of that. Bryant never calls with an emergency."

The moment Von picked up the receiver, the officer yelled, "You and the team need to get to Cole's. Immediately!"

Chapter Three

Dani lurched in her chair at the soft knock against her office doorframe. She glanced up, slamming her laptop shut at the sight of Troy.

"Hey," she muttered. "What's up?"

He entered slowly, eyeing her curiously while balancing a cup of coffee in each hand. "Are you all right? You look like you just saw one of those mummified zombies you used to dream about back when we were kids."

"I'm fine," she lied, still shaken up from the assault outside the Zonian two weeks ago. The lack of leads or suspects only made things worse, as did the alarming comments she'd just read on the Maxwell PD's online forum.

Troy set the coffee on the desk and glanced up at the wall. A satisfied nod preceded his grin of approval.

"What are you cheesing at?" Dani asked.

"That photo of me, you and Chloe at Cole's Ski Resort. Thank you for finally taking down the other one. This is a much better look."

"Don't mention it. Now that you're dating my best friend, I had no choice but to replace the picture with one that represents your new life. Anyway, what's going on? I'm short on time today and need to prep for our community beat meeting."

Taking a seat, Troy pushed aside several piles of paper before propping his elbows onto the desk. "First things first.

What is going on with this office? It isn't like you to be this messy. Normally when I walk in here, everything's in divine order, you're disinfecting the computers, the phone, the drawer handles..."

"I'm just swamped, that's all."

"If you say so. But I'm worried about you, sis. I know you're still recovering from the attack. Yet you refuse to talk to someone."

"Here we go again." Hunching over in her chair, Dani rolled her head, wincing at the pain running across her forehead. She reached for her neck. Ran her fingertips along the faint scars lining her throat. When Troy's eyes tightened in her direction, she tore her hand away and sat straight up. "I appreciate your concern. However, like I said, I'm fine. Please don't worry about me."

"Yeah, well, I don't believe that. Look at you. You're obviously in pain, but you won't go see your doctor. A little therapy would do you some good, too. And this *office*..." Troy swept his arms over the desk like a game show host presenting a prize. "You are the epitome of a neat freak. Yet everything's in disarray. You've got old cups lying everywhere, stacks of reports that need to be filed, unopened mail and boxes piling up. Why don't I see if Chloe can come in and help you get organized—"

"Absolutely not," Dani insisted, tossing a few paper cups in the trash. "I've got everything under control and can have this office looking pristine in no time. As for the pain, I've just got a tension headache. Nothing a couple of ibuprofen can't cure. As a matter of fact..."

Dani ignored the disapproving click of Troy's tongue while reaching inside her drawer and grabbing the bottle. She popped three pills, swallowing them down with a gulp of scalding hot coffee.

"Gah," she gagged, the bitter brew scorching her tongue.

"See? That's what I'm talking about, D. You're off. Your head is all over the place. Let me go and grab you some ice."

"I'm good, Troy. Please. Sit back down and tell me what you need. And make it quick. My meeting's starting soon."

"I know. That's why I came to talk to you. All of Maxwell buzzing about the attack. And everyone knows we don't have any persons of interest to speak of. People are gonna be asking a lot of questions at that meeting and I'm sure they're all worried. How do you want to approach this?"

"Well, first of all, I think the assailant really wanted to scare me and undermine my authority. If that guy wanted me dead, I would be. He attacked me from behind with no warning. I was completely powerless. One or two more tugs from that wire and I'd be dead. And I blame myself for that. I got too comfortable. I should've had my gun in hand. Instead it was tucked away inside my purse, leaving me no chance to defend myself—"

"Dani, don't do that. This was not your fault. You have got to stop blaming yourself. Moving forward, we just have to be more vigilant. More aware of our surroundings. But you're right about the gun thing. Keep it out of your purse and on your hip, whether you're on duty or not."

A soft snicker escaped Dani's lips. She rolled her shoulders as the effects of the pain meds began to kick in.

"What are you snorting about?" Troy asked.

"You. My little brother, whom I still consider to be a rookie cop, giving me advice on how to handle myself."

"But am I wrong?"

"No, you're not wrong at all. And point taken."

Dani picked up her cup, this time blowing into it before taking another sip of coffee. "You still haven't mentioned why you stopped by."

"Have you, um…have you checked the Maxwell PD's website this morning?"

Damn it.

She was hoping to have Chuck, their digital forensics expert, investigate the disturbing comments, remove them discreetly and then present the team with his findings before raising the alarm prematurely.

"I have," she rasped, unable to hide the quiver in her voice.

"So, what are you thinking?"

Anxiety rumbled in the pit of Dani's stomach. She opened her laptop and launched the Maxwell PD's website. A haze of disgust blurred her vision as she reread the comments.

Imagine getting all that attention for catching a killer, just to turn around and get attacked. Chief Miller must feel like a real loser...

Taking all credit for making an arrest when your team actually deserves the accolades is WILD! Serves Chief Miller right that she was almost killed.

I just heard the news that Chief Miller was assaulted. Next time, I hope the attacker finishes the job. Maybe I should step up and do it for him...

The words stung like acid, filling her with a bitter sense of vulnerability.

"I'm so sorry, sis," Troy whispered, his thumbs flying across his cell phone. "I'm texting Chuck now to see if he can delete those comments off the site."

"Thanks. I was planning on doing that right before you came in. And no need to be sorry. We need to be proactive. Find the evidence that'll tie this back to RPS."

Troy fingers froze mid-messaging. "Wait, what are you talking about?"

"Don't tell me you haven't put two and two together. This is the work of Von and his little flunkies."

"And what proof do you have of that?"

"Well, for starters, isn't it funny how Von disappeared from the Zonian right before we left? He had plenty of time to sneak inside my Jeep and lie in wait before he attacked."

Shifting in his chair, Troy bobbed his head, as if contemplating the theory. "I think that's a bit of a reach, don't you? Because again, where's the evidence? And why would Von do something like that? I get that our families aren't on the best of terms. But I don't think it's escalated to the point where he'd assault you."

"You're so naive, Troy. Von *hates* me. He hates all of us. RPS was built on the Reed family's disdain for the Millers. Von's father taught him the inner workings of the crime world—he'd be the perfect criminal. And the motive is obvious. You remember how jealous Von was when we caught the serial killer. He couldn't stand to see Maxwell PD get all that praise."

"Was it Von himself, or some of his officers?"

"Who cares!" Dani exclaimed. "The point is, RPS as a whole is salty and bitter. Since it's Von's company, he's included in that. The man is against me. He's trying to make me pay for my success. For *our* success."

"By viciously attacking you?"

Dani jumped up, her chair slamming against the wall as she paced the cluttered floor. "You don't have to believe me. The truth will eventually reveal itself. It's just a matter of time."

"Well, when it does, I'll be waiting," Troy retorted, catching a box of pepper spray teetering on the edge of the desk. "Until then, we should keep an open mind rather than jump to conclusions."

A knock at the door prevented Dani from arguing any further. "Come in!"

Chuck swung it open, his frizzy red hair blasting from his

scalp like a fireworks display. "Hey, sorry to interrupt. Just wanted to let you know that everything is set up in the conference room for the beat meeting."

"Good, thank you." Dani paused, taking in his gaunt, anxious expression. "What's going on? You don't look like yourself."

"I'm cool. I just wanna make sure you are, too, after seeing those crazy messages on the website."

"I'm fine. Especially since I know who left them." A side-eye from Troy led her to say, "At least I *think* I know. I believe it's the same person who—"

"We should probably head to the conference room, Chief," Troy interrupted, standing before she could finish. "I'm sure the people have a lot to say, and we don't wanna be late."

A stare-down between the siblings commenced, sending Chuck tiptoeing out into the hallway.

"I'll see you two there," he said before jetting off.

Grabbing the agendas off the printer, Dani asked, "So is this what you're doing now? Interrupting your boss while I'm trying to speak with one of my employees?"

"I'd like to think I stopped you from making false accusations."

"I'd like to think of it as me stating my opinion. I'm curious to know what Chuck has to say. What the entire department has to say, actually. Because it's no secret that RPS is out to ruin Maxwell PD's reputation. What better way to do it than to take down the head of the department?"

"I hear you, Dani. But all I'm saying is that in order to back the claim, we've got to have the evidence."

"Thanks for stating the obvious. And that would be nice. But we've scoured the street where the attack took place numerous times and found nothing. My Jeep was thoroughly processed at the lab. Again, nothing. We've watched surveillance footage from every business in the area that had cameras and couldn't make out the suspect. At this point, I wish I could bring Von in for questioning. Find out exactly where he went after leaving the Zonian."

"And on what grounds would you be doing that?"

Breezing past Troy, Dani rolled her eyes. "My suspicions. But you missed the key words. I said 'I wish.' Not 'I will.'"

On the way to the conference room, she noticed a commotion brewing near the front desk as cops rushed out the door. The desk clerk, Natalia, pivoted from side to side, her fluffy blond bob whirling through the air like spinning cotton candy.

"Nat!" Dani said, making a beeline toward her while staring out the window. Officers were hopping inside their cars, flipping on the sirens and flying toward the exit. "What's going on?"

"Chief Miller! I thought you'd already left for Cole's Ski Resort!"

"Why would I be going to Cole's? Our beat meeting starts in a couple of minutes."

"Listen, I was just on the phone with Kelly—"

"Wait, who's Kelly?"

"She's the resort's concierge. While we were talking, I heard all this screaming in the background. I asked what in the world was happening. Apparently, somebody was found injured inside a stairwell. And he might be dead."

"Dead," Dani shot back. "Did she give you any details? Did he get sick? Or was it a fall? Or…something worse?"

"I have no idea. But I did hear someone yell out that they'd seen blood coming from the victim's head."

Dani rocked back on her heels as the air grew thick with tension. A sense of dread engulfed her.

"Troy, can you go and get my things?" she panted before

waving her hand at Natalia. “Go on. Tell me what details came in during the 9-1-1 call.”

“I don’t believe there was a 9-1-1 call. I only knew what was happening because I was on the phone with Kelly. When a few of our officers heard me getting worked up, they jumped into action and headed to the resort.”

“I’m just confused as to why no one called emergency services.”

A flustered Natalia grabbed a nearby file folder and began fanning her face. “I have no idea. Maybe since RPS was already on the scene, everyone thought the situation was under control.”

“Wait, RPS is there?”

“According to Kelly, yes.”

Dani’s head whipped around, her fists clenching as Troy approached with her things. “We need to get to Cole’s. *Immediately.*”

Chapter Four

Von stared down at the victim inside the resort's back stairwell. An excruciating mix of shock and sadness swirled through his chest. Growing up, Cole's had been a second home for him, as his mother was a manager for the beloved establishment. It was still considered one of Maxwell's premier attractions, with tourists visiting from around the world. From the mountain retreat's picturesque timber-framed lodge to its elegant European-inspired furnishings, vacationers enjoyed breathtaking views of the snowcapped peaks and deep valleys surrounding the chalet.

Von had made countless friends there over the years while taking advantage of the various activities. Whether it was skiing, tubing and snowboarding in the winter or golfing, hiking and swimming in the summer, he'd mastered them all.

News of there being a dead body on the scene had sent him reeling. Von braced himself before entering the vestibule, pulling slow, deliberate breaths while studying the victim. It wasn't often that he'd been in the presence of a dead person. The sight was as disturbing as the stench of rotting copper drifting through the tight, stuffy space.

Covering his nose with his hand, Von fought the urge to gag in front of his team. As a leader, the last thing he wanted was to appear weak, as if he lacked the grit to maintain his composure. But seeing the pool of congealed blood splayed beneath the man's head sent his stomach roiling, making it difficult to keep his cool.

The chaos surrounding the scene rang out on the other side of the door, as Von's officers had managed to keep the guests at bay. "Just to confirm, someone did call 9-1-1, right?" he asked for the third time.

"Yes," Officer Bryant huffed. "At least I believe they did. When I ran past the front desk to see what was going on, the concierge was on the phone with law enforcement."

"I wonder why the paramedics aren't here yet? There's only so much our team can do—"

Von broke off mid-sentence when the Maxwell PD stormed through the door like an army of soldiers prepared for combat. Dani led the charge, her slender, curvy silhouette cutting through his officers like a blade. Von watched in awe as she carved a path around her men. Paramedics trailed closely behind, quickly administering aid to the victim.

"Von Reed!" Dani barked.

He stood at attention, as if it were his first day of boot camp. "Yes, Chief Miller?"

"Can you please explain to me why—" The question came to a sudden halt when she glanced down. "Oh my God..." Grabbing hold of Troy, she whispered, "Do you see this?"

"I do," he replied, rubbing his chin.

Von cautiously made his way toward the pair, his eyes darting between them and the victim. "What am I missing? Do you two know the victim?"

Dani and Troy exchanged glances. "I'll get the scene secured," he told her. "Then start up the investigation."

"Good, thank you." Pointing at Von, she said, "You, come with me," before marching up to the second-floor landing.

He followed closely, homing in on her trembling lower lip as she steadied herself against the wall.

"You do know who that is, don't you?" Dani asked.

"According to the guest services manager, his name is Gordon Edwards."

"Right. As in former *Lieutenant* Gordon Edwards. He worked for the Maxwell PD for over three decades before retiring. Lieutenant Edwards was my mentor. That man is one of the main reasons why I'm still on the force. He helped me through some of my toughest times."

Extending an arm, Von murmured, "I'm so sorry, Chief."

She brushed him aside with a dismissive swipe, as if he were a pestering gnat. "Thanks, but I don't need your sympathy. What I need is for you to explain why RPS decided to handle this situation on their own instead of calling 9-1-1."

"We did call 9-1-1. At least that's what Officer Bryant told me. Actually, it was the resort's concierge who made the call."

"*No*, the concierge just so happened to be on the phone with our receptionist. So that's strike one. Here's my next question. How did RPS get here so quickly? Do you have some insider on the premises who thought it would be a good idea to call you instead of the police department?"

"Of course not, Chief. This resort is one of my clients. RPS is here on site every single day."

"So you were here when the incident occurred?"

"No. Officer Bryant was. He's the one who called and told me what was going on."

Dani blew a frustrated sigh while tossing her sandy brown curls into a bun. Her wide-set hazel eyes raced between Von and the floor below as a glimmer of sweat traced the curves of her delicate features. Even in the midst of turmoil, he couldn't help but notice her beauty.

Stop it. Get your head in the game...

"So rather than dial 9-1-1," Dani said, "Officer Bryant calls *you*."

"Yes. Because again, he knew the concierge was reporting the situation to the Maxwell PD. Or at least that's what he thought."

"Okay, let's just end this conversation here since it isn't going anywhere."

Just as Dani grabbed hold of the railing, Von reached for her, gently pulling her back. "Wait, since my team and I were on the scene before you arrived, don't you want to know what we saw? And hear what we think may have happened?"

She hesitated, her right foot hanging over the top stair. A few moments passed before she took a step toward him. "Sure, Von. What are you thinking? Does this look like an accident, or something worse?"

"Oh, something worse, for sure. From what I can tell, it looks as if the victim was shot in the head."

"I cannot believe this," Dani muttered, backing into the wall before doubling over. "It is a nightmare."

Von slowly approached. When she didn't shun him, he rested his hand on her shoulder. This time, she didn't pull away. "You have my condolences."

Shooting up just as quickly as she'd collapsed, Dani ran her palms down the front of her navy blazer and charged back down the stairs. "Look, I need to get to work. Could you please gather up your men and leave my crime scene?"

Are you serious? Von almost blurted before biting down on his jaw. *Just let it go. She's already upset. Don't make it worse.*

Trailing her down the stairs, he heard the paramedic say, "There is nothing more we can do. The victim is deceased."

Von held his breath while awaiting her reaction. Dani responded with a nod, her face crumpling slightly as she motioned to an officer carrying an evidence collection kit. Everyone looked on while he cracked it open, pulling out evidence bags, fingerprint dusting powder, lifting tape and swabs.

"Excuse me," Dani said to Officer Bryant, who was still hovering near the victim. "I'm going to need for you to leave. This is official police business. Plus you're in the way."

Just as the officer puffed out his chest, Von nudged him. "No problem, Chief Miller. Guys, let's give Maxwell PD some space."

Bryant tossed him a look of irritation. Ignoring it, Von headed toward the exit. As much as he wanted to jump in and assist, the chief had spoken. And contrary to what several of his officers wanted to believe, the Maxwell PD took precedence over RPS—especially when it came to crime scenes.

"Excuse me, Officer Bryant?" someone called out from the other side of the cracked door. "Could I speak with you for a minute? I'd like to share some information that might be relevant to what happened here."

The officer swung open the door, replying, "Of course," before stepping into the lobby.

"Hey, hold on!" Dani called out, running after him.

Von followed closely behind in the event he needed to play mediator.

"Mr. Finglass?" Dani said to the man.

"Yes, Chief Miller?" he rasped, pulling nervously at the gray beard hanging from his drooping jowls.

"If you saw something here pertaining to this incident, then you need to report it to the Maxwell PD. *Not* RPS."

"I'd rather not," Mr. Finglass shot back, shrugging his husky shoulders.

"And why is that?" Dani pressed.

"Well, considering how long it took law enforcement to apprehend the killer last year, I'm not convinced your department is capable of handling another murder. So I don't know. Maybe this go-round I should put my trust in RPS. Especially since they were the first officers here on the scene."

"Mr. Finglass," Von said, hoping to quell Dani's frustration as she tossed her hands in the air. "RPS doesn't have the legal authority to work this investigation."

"What do you mean?"

"What he means is," Dani interjected, "the Maxwell PD's legal authority is backed by the U.S. State Government. Therefore, we're the ones who enforce the laws, make arrests, process crime scenes… Do you see where I'm going with this?"

He stood there for several seconds with his jaw suspended in midair. "I—I'm not quite sure that I do."

"You know what…" Dani uttered just as Troy emerged from the stairwell.

He took one look at her asked, "What's going on?"

As she caught him up on the situation, Von turned to Mr. Finglass. "Sir, please. Whatever you wanted to share with RPS, just tell it to Maxwell PD. When it comes to the justice system, they handle the heavy lifting. My company does things like protect private properties and various clients. We don't have the legal clout that the police department does and can't enforce the law like they can. Does that make sense?"

The man's gaze lowered as he slowly uncrossed his arms. "Well, when you put it that way, I guess it does. Who should I talk to?"

Pointing in Dani's direction, Von called out, "Chief Miller? Mr. Finglass is prepared to speak with you now."

"Great. Thank you, sir. I'm going to have you talk to Officer Miller while I have a word with RPS."

"Oh no," Von grumbled under his breath.

Once Troy escorted Mr. Finglass toward a corner of the lobby, Dani approached Officer Bryant. "Would you mind answering a few questions since you were the first one on the scene?"

"I—I uh…"

"Of course he wouldn't mind," Von answered for him, his eyelids twitching with embarrassment. He'd trained his officers to stand up to anyone, and that included the Maxwell PD. "But I would like to stick around while you two talk." When Dani failed to respond, he added, "If that's all right with you, of course." Again, no response. "You know, since Officer Bryant works for my company and all—"

"Fine," Dani relented. "Let's step away from the stairwell and give my officers some space. Plus I'd like to talk in private."

Officer Bryant tossed Von a look of thanks as they followed her through the lobby. When Von saw Dani heading outside, he said, "Bundle up," before zipping his army-green parka.

The threesome tramped through the snow toward the sleigh ride's cedar pergola waiting area. Swirls of flurries whipped through the air, melting against their skin once they stopped underneath infrared lamps hanging from the structure's roof.

Gritting his chattering teeth, Von suppressed the urge to ask why they couldn't talk inside. The lobby's warm English brick fireplace was calling his name. But he already knew how she'd respond. Dani would insist that they needed to speak away from the gawkers. The real answer was that she probably didn't want anyone to see the Maxwell PD mingling with RPS considering they were bitter rivals.

Dani pulled her cell phone from her back pocket and hit the record button. After rattling off the location, date and time, she said, "I've got Officers Reed and Bryant from Reed Protective Services here with me. Officer Bryant was one of the first men on the scene, where former Lieutenant Gordon Edwards was found dead inside the resort's back stairwell. It appears as if he sustained a gunshot wound to the left temple. Officer Bryant, can you please tell me what happened from the moment you were informed that this incident had occurred?"

"Yeah, I uh, I..." His weight shifted from right to left as he peered over at Von.

"Go on," Von insisted, his brows lifting expectantly as he encouraged him to speak.

"So, I was actually patrolling the area right outside of Cole's Sweet Shop when I heard screams coming from inside the main lodge. I made a run for it, charging through the lobby and pushing my way past the crowd that had gathered. It was actually a maintenance guy who found the body—"

"A maintenance guy?" Dani interrupted. "Do you know his name?"

"Mr. Stallworth, I believe."

"Got it. I'll be sure to speak with him. Now at what point did you conclude that the Maxwell PD had been contacted?"

"When I was sprinting past the concierge desk. That's when I overheard Kelly retelling the story and asking if the police were on the way."

Von held a hand in the air, interjecting, "Which could easily explain how Officer Bryant assumed 9-1-1 had been called. He had no idea that Kelly just so happened to be on the phone with your receptionist."

"Duly noted," Dani said.

Studying her stoic expression, Von couldn't tell if she really believed them. But it was obvious that she wasn't in the mood for questions. So he stood down and let her continue.

"What happened next?" she asked.

"When I reached the stairwell, I immediately began performing CPR on the victim. Then one of my partners stepped in who used to work as an EMT. While he administered chest compressions, I called Von. During that time, the victim was unresponsive."

"What about Cole's ski patrol EMTs?" Dani pressed. "Did anybody think to call them?"

"According to the staff, they were on the other side of the mountain treating a skier who'd been in an accident."

Von looked on as Dani's jaw clenched. He braced himself, expecting her to come undone. But instead she held her composure, urging Officer Bryant to continue with a flick of her wrist.

"So then my coworker pulled the cardiac defibrillator from the wall cabinet and tried using that, but it didn't work. The victim remained unresponsive. Soon after, your team arrived, along with paramedics."

"And as far as you could tell, the victim was already deceased when you got to the stairwell?"

"As far as I could tell, yes."

Grief took hold of Dani's somber expression as she turned away, her despondent gaze fixated on the snowy landscape. Once again, Von was hit with the need to comfort her. To assure her that everything would be okay. But he didn't dare try. Instead he stood there. Watching her stare into the distance. As if the pieces to solving the puzzle were hidden in the frosty terrain.

Regaining her composure, Dani spun around, a rekindled fire burning behind her eyes. "Is there anything else can you think of that might help us with this case, Officer Bryant?"

"Hmm, I think that's it."

"Okay then. Well, if something comes to mind, no matter how small, you know where to find me."

"I do."

As Dani set off toward the lodge, Von quickly added, "I'll do the same. And we'll all be sure to keep our antennas up in case any other intel emerges, whether it be around my office or out in the streets."

"You sure about that?" Dani asked over her shoulder.

"Of course I'm sure. Why wouldn't I be?"

She skidded to a sudden stop. Her hunter-green boots kicked up a cloud of snow that whirled around them. A few of the flurries landed on her lush lips.

Look away...

But he didn't, instead fixating on the flakes as they melted into her pink gloss. The visual activated a deep stirring sensation.

You need to leave, his told himself. *Just walk off.*

That feeling he felt was all too familiar. It didn't come around often. But when it did, he knew exactly what it meant. Strong desire, and innate attraction, toward whoever was standing in front of him.

"Officer Reed," Dani spat, "have you forgotten about the long-standing, toxic history between the Maxwell PD and RPS? To put it nicely, your company hasn't always been upfront when it comes to sharing intel with my department."

Von's lips parted. But nothing came out. He wanted to speak. Yet didn't quite know what to say. Because Dani was absolutely right.

A long stretch of silence ensued. Nothing could be heard beyond the eerie whistling winds swirling through the icy peaks.

"Excuse me," Officer Bryant said, "but um, Von? Should I excuse myself and let you two talk, or…whatever this is you're doing?"

"Yes," Von told him without taking his eyes off of Dani. "I think that would be a good idea." Once the crunch of snow beneath the officer's feet grew faint, Von stepped in closer. "Chief Miller, would you mind elaborating on that statement you just made?"

"I wouldn't mind at all. You do recall the various ways in which RPS has attempted to interfere in a number of past investigations, don't you?"

"Actually, no. I can't seem to recall that at all."

"So, you don't recall the rumors that were going around about how you and your employees were gathering leads on potential suspects linked to my cases, but weren't sharing them with the police department?"

"Once again, no. I do not."

As Dani moved in, her arms crossed tightly over her chest, Von inhaled a hint of citrus drifting from her neck. He swiveled slightly, hoping to avoid another whiff of the intoxicating aroma.

"Welp," she snipped, "fortunately for you, my memory does serve me correctly. I can recall all the ways in which RPS has tried to sabotage my cases. I'm pretty sure we both know why, too."

"Speak for yourself, because I'm completely clueless. Why don't you enlighten me?"

Dani let off a patronizing chuckle that misted through the air. "Von, when it comes to prior cases, you and your guys were always so desperate to catch my suspects and claim all the glory. You'd go behind our backs and interview alleged witnesses. Sneak onto crime scenes after hours to try to collect evidence. Call the forensics lab, trying to get test results. I should've arrested all of you for obstruction of justice, witness tampering *and* interfering with our investigations. The sad thing is, I wouldn't be surprised if your father was the one encouraging your criminal behavior."

"Chief Miller, those guys you're referring to were never official RPS employees. I'd hired them on a contractual basis to work a couple of events when I was understaffed. That's it. And as for my father, please don't bring him into this."

"Oh, it's a little too late for that. He brought himself into it. Back when my father was running the police department, Maxwell's criminal justice system was still of one accord. But then once your dad launched RPS, all hell broke loose. Things haven't been the same since. I actually wouldn't be surprised if RPS was stirring all this up in an attempt to take down the force. The attack on me, the vile messages left on Maxwell PD's website, Lieutenant Edwards's murder…"

Dani's biting words burned away the numbness of the cold, leaving Von seething in his stance. "Hold on. You really think that RPS is behind all this?"

"I'm just saying that it wouldn't surprise me if you were—"

"Yeah, I think we're done here," Von interrupted, his Timberland boots pounding the snow as he backed away. "I don't know what you're going through, Chief Miller, but you're losing it. Which is sad, considering I could be an asset to you. But I'm not gonna stand here and let you take your frustrations out on me. However, I will tell you this. When it comes to these crimes? You need to take your focus off of RPS. If you don't, you'll never solve the case."

Chapter Five

"Trust me," Dani said to Chloe and Troy, "I went off on Von so bad that there is no going back. At this point, he and I are enemies for life."

The three of them were sitting out on Dani's backyard deck, sipping wine and preparing dinner while watching the sun set. The yard had become a sanctuary of sorts, a place where she could unwind after long, hectic days.

She settled against her chair's red cedar frame, listening to melodic calls of northern mockingbirds. Her eyes followed the smoke drifting from the grill as it disappeared into her desert willow tree. The instant her lids lowered, visions of Lieutenant Edwards's dead body flashed through her mind like lightning, disrupting the moment of peace.

Over a week had passed since his murder, and no viable leads had emerged. The only DNA found near the scene belonged to the lieutenant. There were no fingerprints, foreign materials or identifiable secretions that could be traced back to the crime.

The lack of evidence cast a somber cloud over the department. Dani worked tirelessly to keep the morale afloat. But as each day went by with no new clues, fear began to drown out any remaining hope. The once-bustling energy around the station transformed into oppressive silence. The usual chatter and lighthearted updates morphed into clacking keyboards, muffled phone calls and a team on edge, desperate for a break.

But no one carried the pressure quite like Dani. While the police department worked as a whole, she was their leader. The expectations placed on her were greater. And the burden of every failure was hers to bear.

Dani's deepening concern over the recent murder left her confined to her desk, mulling over the case for hours on end. It had gotten so bad that Troy insisted she pull herself away and come home early for a home-cooked meal. Since she didn't have the energy to boil an egg, she'd agreed. And now, as the savory scent of halibut, Greek potatoes and roasted asparagus drifted through the air, Dani was glad she did.

"Personally?" Chloe said while refilling their glasses. "I don't blame you for going off on Von. However, you did *kind of* accuse the man of being a criminal, so…there's that."

"I said what I said. And I meant it. I wouldn't put anything past Von or any of his guys. It really pissed him off when I threw his father into the conversation. Being that he's such a daddy's boy, he'd do anything to please that man. And nothing would appease Old Man Reed more than taking down the Maxwell PD."

"Seriously, Dani?" Troy interjected. "You really think Von and his father are killers?"

"They could be," Dani insisted, stomping her bare foot against the mahogany planks. "Those men have huge egos. They'd do anything to shine a positive light on themselves and boost their business. Look at how Mr. Reed treated Dad back in the day. He left our father high and dry when he needed him the most. I know firsthand what it feels like to be a young new police chief. Your officers are all you've got. So to be betrayed and abandoned like that is beyond hurtful."

"Well, not to defend him or anything, but Mr. Reed was

hurt, too. He thought that Dad was being too hard on him, and I'm sure having to take orders from a friend was tough. Also, I don't even think our fathers hate each other like they used to. So much time has passed, it seems to be more like indifference these days than anything. But the bottom line is that I just don't think the Millers are killers." Tossing Chloe a wink, he added, "See what I did there?"

Shifting in her chair, Dani stared Troy down as he raised the top on the grill. "Troy, please. *Focus*. And I'm sorry, but whose side are you on?"

"Yours, of course. Which is why I can't stand here and lie to you. You've got to think rationally. I won't be convinced that RPS is involved in these crimes until I see some evidence that's directly linked to them."

"Best friend," Dani said to Chloe, "please step in and have my back on this. Do you think I'm wrong?"

"Well..."

"Oh, so now both of you are ganging up on me?" Grabbing her cell, Dani scrolled through the contacts. "I should call up some of my officers and talk to them instead of you two. Clearly I need to surround myself with more like-minded individuals."

Chloe threw her napkin over her head and waved it in the air. "Okay, okay, I surrender. Put the phone down, and let's seriously talk suspects. Aside from RPS, who else do you think may have wanted Lieutenant Edwards dead?"

"It could've been one of our officers," Troy suggested. "Not to throw Maxwell PD under the bus or anything, but think about how angry some of them were when you became police chief. Lieutenant Edwards was critical in you landing that job."

"That's true," Dani agreed. "But I just can't see someone on our squad being bitter enough to kill a retired lieutenant, just to get back at me."

"I can."

"Unfortunately," Chloe cut in, "so can I. This could be their way of getting back at the person who helped you, *and* burdening you with yet another murder investigation. Add in the attack and those messages on Maxwell PD's website, it could all be a ploy to get you to quit, which may be what they ultimately want."

Pulling her knees to her chest, Dani stared down at the plate of food that Troy set in front of her. "You know, when I think back on the day I got promoted, it was so bittersweet. I was thrilled, of course. So were a lot of my fellow officers. There were definitely those who weren't, though. But never in my wildest dreams did I imagine all this would come with the job."

"Who would?" Troy asked, handing Chloe her plate, then taking a seat. "If we're naming names here, I'd say Kenin, Henderson and Simons should be at the top of your list of haters." There was a noticeable tremor in Troy's hands as he cut into his potatoes. "*Damn.* I really do hate that we're even having this conversation. But it's a sad reality that we have to consider."

The sting of betrayal soured Dani's appetite as she pushed her plate away. Chloe, her expression softening, said, "Here's a thought. Maybe Lieutenant Edwards's murder was a personal attack that had nothing to do with the Maxwell PD *or* RPS."

"We've considered that," Dani said. "His ski club partners were there the day he was killed. They've all been cleared. We talked to his family. His wife said she was with friends that afternoon, and they backed that claim. Their oldest son, Martin, was at work. But…"

"But what?" Chloe asked.

"We're still looking into their youngest son, Evan. He has gotten into some trouble in the past. Drug-related. Lieutenant Edwards was pretty hard on him, right along with his dealer, who just so happened to be Evan's best friend. The dealer ended up doing time while Evan was sent to rehab."

"So you're thinking those two could be behind the murder?"

"It's a possibility. We're still working to verify their alibis. They were allegedly on a road trip to Orange County to visit a marijuana megastore that recently opened. Chuck already reached out to the store's security team to request surveillance footage. They haven't responded yet. If we don't hear back soon, we'll get Vista Del Sol's police department involved, then go from there."

"Here's a thought," Troy said before downing a mouthful of food. "Maybe the lieutenant's murder was a random act of violence."

"Could be..." As Dani settled into the conversation, she reached for her fork and stabbed at a stalk of asparagus. Hunger pangs hit after the first bite. "Mmm, this is so good, Troy."

"Thanks. I'm glad we're doing this..." His voice drifted as crinkles framed his downcast gaze. "There's something else I've been thinking about. And I hope I'm wrong about this, but it could be that we're dealing with a copycat killer here."

Dani winced at the thought, chasing it down with a long gulp of wine. "That would be a nightmare. It's actually crossed my mind more than once, but I'm not dwelling on it. My focus is on catching the killer before another murder occurs."

"*If* another murder occurs," Chloe said. "Let's hope this was just an isolated incident. Did the surveillance footage from Cole's security team reveal anything?"

"No, unfortunately. So many of the guests were walking around wearing ski masks, helmets and goggles, which made it almost impossible to ID them. Another thing I've been thinking about is if there were other witnesses who saw something and withheld it from us so they could pass it along to RPS, like Mr. Finglass attempted to do."

"Let's hope not," Troy said, reaching for a second helping of potatoes. "I can't imagine anyone would wanna play those types of games in this situation. Not after everything we went through. As for Finglass, I'd hate to call the man a liar, but his recollection of what he *thought* he saw was completely off. The bloody palm print he claimed to have spotted near the stairwell was a red arrow painted on the wall. Then the alleged argument he'd sworn he saw the lieutenant having with a ski instructor never happened. Edwards and his ski crew rented a private slope and no instructor had gone near the area. Finglass probably saw him talking to one of his guys."

"Yeah," Dani said, running her hand along the back of her stiff neck. "He just wanted some attention and accolades. On another note, I have got to stop sitting behind my desk so much and get some exercise. My entire body feels like it's been dipped in cement I am so stiff." Stopping mid-sentence, she reached over and nudged Chloe's arm. "Weren't we supposed to be signing back up for Spin classes this fall?"

"We were. I'm still waiting on you to tell me whether you wanna be on the Monday, Wednesday, Friday schedule, or Tuesday, Thursday, Saturday. So the ball's in your court, friend."

"Let me check my calendar tomorrow and get back to you."

"That's what she told me two months ago," Chloe muttered to Troy.

"I heard that," Dani quipped. "I need to figure out the next steps in this investigation. My entire squad is on edge. And they're getting discouraged by the lack of evidence and leads. I've gotta do something to lift their spirits. Keep them motivated."

Troy stood and began clearing their plates. "Let's get aggressive then. Show the team that we're doing everything we can to solve this thing. We'll go back to Cole's and question the staff again. Drive out to Vista Del Sol and talk to the security team about that surveillance footage in person. Try to get a hold of Cole's maintenance guy again who discovered Lieutenant Edwards's body. I still think it's strange how he left the resort before we had a chance to really question him, and he hasn't been back to work since."

"I don't think he's our guy," Dani countered. "Officer Shields spoke to him briefly before he clocked out. I watched the body cam footage, and he was so shaken up that he could barely talk. Didn't seem like it was an act, either. And as far as him taking time off work goes, who can blame him? The man is probably traumatized."

"Well, when you put it that way..."

"Plus there was nothing at the scene that would indicate he was involved. He didn't have any blood on him, there was no weapon found in his possession, and his DNA didn't turn up anywhere near the scene or on the body."

Chloe emitted an ominous moan while pouring the last of the wine. "I'm about to say something that neither of you want to hear."

"Which is?" Dani asked.

"Back when I was working for the Chicago PD, any time we had a murder scene with no evidence left behind, we'd just have to wait it out. See if the killer would strike again. And hope that next time, he'd slip up and leave a trail of evidence."

"Hmph..." Dani pulled herself up from the table. "I think I need more wine. While I grab a bottle, I'm gonna call the head of the crime lab again. Ask her to go over the results one more time, just to make sure she didn't miss anything. I can't sit back and wait for another body to turn up. This isn't another random case to me. It's personal. And when I think about these recent crimes, one thing comes to mind—I may be next."

Chapter Six

Von downed the last of his whiskey sour while staring at his phone. He and Kevin had just left a meeting with the Maxwell Historical Society to finalize security details for a high-profile exhibit opening, and swung by the Zonian for drinks before calling it a night.

It had been a long, hectic few weeks since the death of Lieutenant Edwards. RPS had been bombarded with security requests, and a wave of tension had gripped the town.

"I wonder what's going on with the Maxwell PD," Kevin said. "I haven't heard a thing about Lieutenant Edwards's case. Are there any leads? Suspects? Persons of interest? *Anything?*"

"I have no clue. But I haven't heard anything, either. When I think back on Dani's attitude at the crime scene, I'm sure she wants to keep it that way. At least when it comes to me. That woman hates my guts."

"Yeah, well, that's on her. You had every right to be at Cole's that day."

"It wasn't just the fact that I was there," Von said. "Somehow wires got crossed, and Maxwell PD wasn't immediately called when the victim's body was found. So Dani assumed that RPS was trying to investigate the scene on our own and purposely exclude the police department. That thought process led to her mentioning my father, then next thing I know, *boom*, she's accusing me of murder."

"Wait, *what*? I didn't know she took it that far."

Signaling the bartender, Von gestured that he needed a refill. "I'm telling you, Kev, our rivalry runs deep. So deep that I don't think *I* even realized how bad it was until now."

"But to accuse you of killing a man? Come on. *You*, a man whose father was on the force, who took over the family business and now works to keep people safe. Not to mention you volunteer with youth programs and look out for your elderly neighbors. You're probably the nicest guy I know!" Shaking his head in disgust, Kevin muttered, "I still don't understand what you see in that woman."

"What do you mean? I see in her what everybody else sees."

Rolling his head back, Kevin blew a rumbling grunt. "Ohh no you don't. Now before I get started, I will say this. Dani is attractive. But I can't name a man in this town who's actually attracted *to* her, other than you."

"Ha!" Von snorted so loudly that it turned a few heads. He ignored them while pushing Kevin's old-fashioned out of reach. "I think you may have had a little too much to drink, my friend. Because *me*, attracted to Dani? What in the hell would make you say something like that?"

"How about the fact that it's true? Do you really think you're inconspicuous enough to hide your feelings for her? Seriously, you've has a crush on her since elementary school—"

"Now *that* is a bold-faced lie."

"Is it though? Von, let's not forget that I'm your closest friend. I know you better than you know yourself. Plus, I see the way you look at Dani whenever she's around. The way you get all soft acting whenever she speaks to you, even if she's being rude as hell. Go on and admit it. You admire the woman. As a matter of fact, I think you're in love with her."

"Okay, now you're taking it way too far. Even if I did feel

a little something toward her, it wouldn't matter. Thanks to our fathers, she is completely off-limits."

"But not once have you said you wouldn't want to be with her."

When Von broke eye contact and thanked the bartender for his drink, Kevin slid his phone in front of him.

"On another note, have you seen this?" he asked, enlarging the top story on *The Maxwell Times*'s website.

"No, I haven't," Von said before scanning the headline.

"Maxwell PD's Message Board Hit with Threats Against Police Chief."

"Damn. I'm reading through the threats now…"

Police Chief Danielle Miller thinks she's a hotshot for solving that big murder case. Let's see whether it was a fluke, or if she can catch me, too.

Hey, Chief Miller! Be on the lookout, because I'm watching youuu. And when I get you, it won't be pretty.

I hope the chief enjoys being tied up and detained, because I've got a special spot in my basement waiting for her...

Dread twisted inside Von's gut. He turned away, taking another long sip of his drink while thinking back on his conversation with Dani at the crime scene. It suddenly made sense why she was so defensive. The woman was probably terrified.

"That's pretty brutal," Kevin said. "I may not be too fond of Dani, but she doesn't deserve all that."

"I agree. I almost wanna call and see if she's okay. She has gone through so much hell already, and it's terrible that she's the focus of this misguided hate."

"Same. But do you really think Dani would want to hear from you? Especially if she thinks you're her suspect?"

"I don't know. If I had to guess, probably not. That doesn't mean I can't reach out in a show of support. What's happening here goes way beyond some ridiculous beef and her wild accusations. This is real. The woman's life is in danger. Not to mention Dani runs the police department. Like them or not, RPS is almost a subdivision of the force."

Kevin let off a dry chuckle while swirling the ice in his glass. "Yeah, maybe in your mind. But in reality, the Maxwell PD looks at us as being some substandard watchdog group, even though we're far from that. We are the gold standard of security firms. We're elite and highly trained, our clientele is ultraexclusive, and we provide the ultimate level of protection. Yet the police department continues to disrespect us."

"But that disrespect didn't start with us. We inherited it. So maybe it could end with us, you know? Dani and I don't have to keep fueling the fire that our fathers started. We could be the ones to put it out, and work to unite RPS and Maxwell PD."

"Good luck with that," Kevin retorted, turning his attention toward a group of women walking through the door. "Uh-oh…"

"Uh-oh, what?"

"Don't turn around."

"Why not?"

"Because your ex just walked in."

"Ugh," Von groaned, ducking his head in the other direction. "Which one?"

"That hostess you were seeing who works at Vortex Lounge. What's her name? Marissa? Miranda?"

"Melody," Von corrected through tight lips.

"Yeah, Melody." Spinning on his stool, Kevin blew a low whistle. "Damn, man. I'm sorry, but she looks gorgeous, too."

Cutting his eyes over his shoulder, Von watched as Melody navigated her way through the crowd with ease. She relished the attention she drew, blowing air kisses to her admirers while swaying her lithe dancer's physique to the beat of the music. There was no denying her allure—the flawless raven pixie cut, radiant makeup, sexy black lace catsuit… But Melody's entire personality was built on her beauty, which had been a huge turnoff for Von.

"Tell me again why you two broke up?" Kevin asked.

"First of all, will you please turn back around before she sees us? I am not in the mood to answer a bunch of questions about where I've been and why I haven't called her. Secondly, there was no breakup. She and I didn't even date for a whole month."

Turning toward the bar, Kevin elbowed Von in the chest. "Quit being coy and answer the question. Why did you cut ties with her?"

"Long story short, she was too young for me. I didn't realize she was only twenty-four when I asked her out."

"Dude, haven't you heard? Age ain't nothing but a number."

"Yeah," Von huffed, "but not in her case. Melody was too superficial for my taste. Plus she runs the streets too much. She worked all hours of the night at the lounge, and when she wasn't there, she was out partying everywhere else."

"Nah, that's not it. You just don't wanna settle down."

"I wouldn't say all that. I'm just a busy man. I'm running a company and don't have much free time. But aside from not really being in a position to settle down, I don't want to settle. Why get involved with someone who I'm not really feeling?"

"You've got a point. But hey, don't pay too much attention to me. I don't know what's going on out here. I've been married and off the streets for a long time."

Von leaned in, raising his voice over the blaring techno music. "Yeah, you got lucky and found a good one right out of college. Some of us are still out here searching for our soulmates."

"At this point, you shouldn't be. You've met plenty of amazing women that you passed up for whatever reason. My wife and I alone have played matchmaker more times than I can count. But nobody's ever good enough for the great Von Reed. And I think I know why."

"Aww, here we go. I'm not even gonna take the bait."

Gripping his shoulder, Kevin replied, "You don't have to. I'll say it loud and clear. You're holding out for Dani."

"All right..." Von pushed away from the bar, his awkward chuckle masking the realization that he hadn't concealed his feelings as well as he'd thought.

"Oh no," Kevin grunted. "Brace yourself."

"For what?"

"Melody and her girls are making their way over here."

"Damn it. I should've left when I had the chance."

Von's muscles tensed as a slender hand drifted across the small of his back.

"Heyyy, Von-Von," Melody murmured in his ear.

Discreetly recoiling from her touch, he replied, "Hey, how's it going?"

"It's going well. But it would be even better if you'd buy me a drink, then explain why you haven't called me."

A fitting response eluded Von as he stood there, his mouth gaping and mind suddenly going blank.

"Aww, that's so cute," Melody purred, her sticky lip gloss clinging to his lobe. "I've rendered you speechless."

"No, you just caught me off guard, that's all. I didn't expect to see you here."

"Well, now that you're seeing me," she said, spinning a slow 360-degree turn, "and you've had a few moments to think, answer the question. Why haven't I heard from you?"

"For starters, work has been crazy. And remember how we talked about this the last time we went out? I'm not really dating right now."

"Sweetheart, haven't you heard? *Nobody* is too busy for Melody Anderson."

Von tossed a wad of cash on the bar, caught Kevin's attention, and motioned toward the exit. "Listen, Melody. It was nice seeing you, but I just don't think I'm what you're looking for. I'm sure there are plenty of guys who'd love to take you out—"

"Oh, trust me, I already know. I've got several of them on the roster. But nobody puts Melody to the side and gets away with it. You need to call me and get back in the starting lineup."

"Yeah, well, I'll pass. Have a good night. Kev, let's go."

"Right behind you, boss."

"Your loss!" Melody called out.

Von responded with a brusque wave, his eyes meeting hers as she stared him down on his way to the exit.

Chapter Seven

Dani strolled the produce aisle of Golden Canyon Grocers, debating whether to purchase another bag of apples after she'd let the last batch spoil.

"Leave it," she muttered, opting for a bag of pears instead.

Turning her cart in the opposite direction, she headed toward the hot bar and perused the array of dishes. While the rich, tangy scents of sweet-and-sour salmon, chicken Parmesan, and teriyaki shrimp sent her empty stomach rumbling, Dani kept walking. She had been to the store just the day before and hadn't returned because she'd forgotten something. She was back, avoiding the emptiness of her house.

It had been more than a month since Lieutenant Edwards's murder, yet she was no closer to identifying a suspect. Meanwhile, the threats against Dani not only persisted, but they were growing increasingly ominous. She had yet to tell anyone about the strange phone calls she'd been getting. Earlier that afternoon, her cell phone rang nonstop hour after hour while she was at the station. *Private Caller* or *Anonymous* flashed across the screen each time. When she'd answer, whoever was on the other end didn't say a word. But their deep, guttural breathing, which sometimes transformed into animalistic grunts, could be heard loud and clear.

Dani had every intention of turning the phone over to Chuck for analysis. But she already knew the number would probably be untraceable. Anyone bold enough to harass the chief of police would know better than to leave a digital trail. Nevertheless, she was obligated to pursue every possible lead.

Just when she reached the sushi bar, Dani heard someone call out her name.

"Chief Miller!" he repeated when she didn't acknowledge him the first time.

"Yes?" she said, twirling her cart around even though she was in no mood to socialize.

"I've been meaning to reach out to you. How have you been?"

Dani's fingers clutched the handle tighter, her eyes flashing with annoyance at the sight of Von.

"I'm fine. And you?" she said coolly, turning her attention to a row of sashimi.

"I'm hanging in there. Honestly, I'm still pretty disturbed by Gordon Edwards's murder."

"Are you really?" Dani shot back, her flat voice tinged with skepticism.

"Yes, of course. Officer Bryant is pretty shaken up, too, which is understandable since he was one of the first officers on the scene. I'm sure that Maxwell PD is working diligently on the investigation. Have there been any new leads, or—"

"How's your phone doing?" she interrupted, pointing toward Von's cell.

"It's—it's fine. Why?"

"Oh, I was just wondering. I'm surprised it isn't overheating, or on fire, actually."

Von held up the phone, his wide eyes shifting rapidly between it and Dani. "Um… I'm not quite sure what you're getting at, but like I said, my phone is fine."

"Yeah, okay. Maybe that one is. What about the other one?"

"*What* other one?"

"Your burner phone."

"Chief Miller, I have no idea where you're going with this, but I don't have a burner phone, and the cell that I do have is good. Anyway, sorry I bothered you. I'll let you get back to your shopping—"

"You think I'm an idiot, don't you?"

Von stopped so abruptly that his sneakers' soles screeched along the tile. "*No*, of course I don't. But I am starting to question your mental state."

Dani yanked her phone from her purse and stepped aggressively into Von's space. She froze when his biceps pressed against her breasts, shocked by the tingling sensation shooting through her chest.

Edging back, her eyes locked on the cell while Von's lingered on her. "Trust me, I'm perfectly sane. Which is surprising considering I've been harassed all afternoon. Do you see this?" she screeched as her thumb scrolled down the screen. "Call after call from anonymous or private numbers. When I'd answer, some maniac was on the other end, breathing a crazed animal." Dani's gaze darkened, rising to meet Von's. "Isn't it interesting that this started right after our confrontation at Cole's? And you're expecting me to believe you know nothing about it?"

"Yes. That's exactly what I'm expecting. Because it's the truth. And I'm sorry all this is happening to you, Chief. But please believe me when I tell you I have nothing to do with any of it."

"I'm sorry, but I'm just not convinced. If it isn't you, then it's probably someone from your company. Somebody who can't get past the bad blood between us."

Von leaned in closer, his husky voice low and riddled with irritation. "All right then, prove it. Show me the evidence that backs your claims. I already know you can't. And that you're grasping at straws. You obviously have no leads. You can't even name a person of interest. So you're taking the easy route and blaming your shortcomings on my company."

Pushing her cart aside, Dani spun around and set off in the opposite direction. "I may not have the evidence yet, but it's just a matter of time. I'll figure it out. I always do."

"Chief Miller," Von called out, following her toward the exit. *"Chief Miller!"*

She ignored him, almost getting hit by a car while running through the parking lot. When she got to her Jeep, Dani stopped so suddenly that she almost fell against the hood.

The windshield had been completely smashed, its center appearing like a warped spiderweb as shards of glass hung from the frame. All of the tires were violently slashed. The burgundy paint was scraped away in jagged lines with what appeared to be a knife. Deep cuts revealed the raw metal underneath, leaving gashes that tore through the finish.

"Oh my God," Dani moaned, her weakening legs threatening to fold as she charged back inside the store.

Von, who was hovering near the entrance, tried to stop her. "Chief Miller, what's going on?"

She rushed right past him and continued toward the customer service desk.

"I need to speak to the manager," she told the attendant. "Now! And where is your security officer? Is he on duty?"

"He's right behind you, ma'am."

Pulling out her badge, Dani attempted to introduce herself to the guard. He stopped her mid-sentence.

"Chief Miller, we all know who you are around here. You're our local hero. Or is it heroine? Hey, Maggie?" he said to the attendant. "Should I refer to Chief Miller as Maxwell's hero, heroine, or—"

"Sir," Dani interrupted. "Thank you, but please, I need

your help. Someone vandalized my car while I was inside the store. Could I take a look at the surveillance footage covering the parking lot?"

"Of course. I—I'm so sorry. Follow me."

While Dani made her way to the back of the store, she called Troy. The conversation was disrupted by the sound of approaching footsteps. Dani turned and saw Von trailing her, his eyes fixed intently on her.

"Hold on, Troy," she said into the phone before pressing it against her chest. "Von, what are you doing?"

"I'm coming with you. I saw what someone did to your car out there, and I didn't wanna leave you alone while you review the footage."

"That won't be necessary. My brother is on his way, and several other officers should be here shortly."

"Are you sure?"

"Of course I'm sure."

"Okay, well, the good news is, when this happened, you had eyes on me, so…" He hesitated, as if waiting on Dani to respond. She remained silent. "What I'm trying to say is, this proves that I'm not the one committing these crimes against you."

Dani ended the call with Troy, then stood in the control room doorway. "Von, while I review this footage and attempt to identify the suspect, why don't you go back to RPS headquarters. Check in with your staff. See if you can figure out where each of your employees was during this past hour."

"Okay, so now you're insinuating that one of my employees vandalized your—"

Before he could finish, Dani shut the door in his face.

Chapter Eight

"I tried, Chief," Chuck said on the other end of the phone. "Trust me, I couldn't have dug much deeper. There just wasn't enough information available that could prove where the threats are coming from."

Dani swiveled on her cream barstool as she shifted between two open laptops, her personal cell phone and a stack of case file folders. Her kitchen had undergone a radical transformation, evolving from a warm, inviting space to a cutting-edge command center. She'd set up her devices along the beige granite island, with the Maxwell PD's message board displayed on one computer, her email inbox on the other, and the anonymous text thread open on her cell.

A dull ache pulsated throughout Dani's entire body. The numbing pain kicked in the moment she sat down and began reading through the scathing statements made against her. Each comment, each threat, left her agonizing over who was behind it all.

She'd been sure that Chuck would uncover some sort of lead. A digital trail, a cell tower's ping…anything that might point them in the direction of their suspect. But the perpetrator knew what they were doing. And if their goal was to incite fear in Dani, it was working.

After the run-in with Von at the grocery store, Dani found herself rethinking his involvement. She couldn't shake the feeling that his concern for her seemed genuine. And then there was the fact that her vehicle had been vandalized while he was inside. While he may not have done it, she couldn't rule out the possibility that one of his cohorts was behind it. Whether or not Von was the mastermind remained to be seen.

"So hold on," Dani said to Chuck. "What happened when you traced those comments on the Maxwell PD's message board? Were you able to pull the IP addresses?"

"No, unfortunately. The users must've hidden them using a virtual private network. In some cases, these people are using double VPNs, which makes it even harder for their internet activity to be tracked."

Dani's head fell against her palm as she squeezed her temples in frustration. "What about the anonymous calls and text messages? Any luck tracing those?"

"No, and for similar reasons. The caller is either using a burner phone with a prepaid SIM card, or the phone's data is encrypted using a VPN."

"This is so damn aggravating," she said just as her phone beeped. Natalia's name flashed across the screen. Dani's stomach dropped when she saw the call was coming from the police station.

"Chuck, I'll call you back." She almost dropped the phone while fumbling to swap calls. "Nat, what's going on?"

"Chief, something's going down at the Blanche Hotel. I don't know all the details, but there's been some sort of incident. And I think it's fatal."

DANI TORE DOWN Rockfield Road, her siren blaring through the still desert air. The Blanche Hotel stood on the east end of downtown Maxwell. Several of her officers were already on the scene, as Mayor Cox had asked the department to keep an eye on things during his high-profile fundraising event.

The hotel's iconic red sign flickered steadily in the distance. Built in the 1930s, the Blanche had become quite a popular tourist attraction, second only to Cole's Ski Resort. Its terra-cotta-tiled roof, golden beige stucco walls and gracefully arched windows mixed timeless Italian elegance with old-world charm, earning the establishment a loyal following.

The beauty of the hotel diminished under the circumstances as Dani's black Ford sedan skidded to a halt, narrowly missing the colorful flower beds lining the cobblestoned driveway. Panic throbbed against her forehead at the familiarity of it all. Like the other crime scenes, this one hit like a violent storm. Blue and red lights flashed in the distance. Sirens cracked through the dark quiet. The imminent tragedy she'd soon face lingered in the air.

Without waiting for her officers to pull up, Dani jumped out of the car and charged the lobby. Partygoers' faces were a blur in the sea of madness. She almost collided with several of them as the dark woodwork and dimly lit sconces made it impossible to see through the turmoil. Footsteps pounded the glossy terrazzo tiles, each step growing more frantic than the last as attendees scrambled in every direction.

Dani climbed the stairs leading the grand ballroom two at a time. The commotion heightened as flustered guests draped in designer gowns and tailored tuxedos struggled to make sense of the scene.

The moment she approached the ballroom's vaulted entryway, Dani paused at the sound of a deep, familiar voice, vibrating through the air.

"Everyone, please! Listen up! Stay calm, and head down to the lobby using the staircase to your left. The elevators are to your right."

Von...

"What in the hell is RPS doing here?" Dani asked Troy when he approached.

"I'm not sure, but they seem to be doing a decent job of evacuating the area."

"Yeah, well, it's not good enough. Guests are still charging through the halls, causing chaos. Can you and the team help move everyone down to the lobby? Better yet, let's facilitate a full evacuation. I need them out of the hotel, now."

"You got it, Chief."

The moment Troy stepped away, Dani cut through the crowd and headed straight to Von.

"Once again," she said, "I see RPS beat me to the scene. How does this keep happening?"

"My men were already on-site. The mayor hired us to provide security for the event. One of my guys called to let me know what was going on. I just so happened to be close by, so it didn't take me long to get here."

"Wait, why would the mayor hire RPS when he had the Maxwell PD patrolling the event?"

With a slight shrug, Von replied, "Ever since that big crime case, he's been extra cautious, believing that one can never have too much security."

"So what you're telling me is tonight's incident occurred under Maxwell PD's *and* RPS's watch."

"Yes. Which is not a good look…"

Dani pivoted, uncomfortable under Von's intense gaze. "The victim is inside the ladies' restroom, correct?"

"Yes, she is."

"How in the world did someone manage to commit murder with all these people around?"

"The victim was found in a restroom located in the west wing of the hotel. The event is taking place in the east wing."

"Hmm, got it." Pulling a long stream of air, Dani's body

stiffened as she prepared for the worst. "Okay then. Let's walk and talk."

Guests stepped aside when they saw Dani and Von making their way through the crowd. She was careful when responding to their questions, telling everyone she'd share details once she knew more.

"Just keep walking," Von said, placing a hand on her shoulder while guiding her past the inquisitive attendees.

Several moments passed before Dani realized Von was still holding on to her. She surprised herself by not shoving his hand away.

When they arrived near the area where the ladies' room was located, it had already been cordoned off. Von raised the yellow caution tape over Dani's head as she ducked underneath it and entered the gruesome scene. The first thing she noticed was blood spattered along the soft peach wallpaper and white marble floor. The victim's glittery black pumps were sticking out from underneath a row of porcelain pedestal sinks. First responders hovered around her with first aid kits, portable oxygen tank, tourniquets and defibrillator set up nearby.

Dani's lungs restricted as her entire body went numb, cutting off her ability to feel. To breathe. To move.

"Hey, are you good?" Von asked.

The touch of his hand on the small of her back unlocked the traumatic hold on her limbs, pushing her farther inside the restroom.

Pull it together. Do not let this man see you fold...

A mass of blood had pooled beneath the victim's body, soaking her silver sequined gown. Dani's stomach clenched as she approached Officer Rose, their crime scene investigator. "Any initial thoughts? Gunshot wound? Stab wound?"

"Stab wound for sure. It looks to be several from what the

paramedics are saying. Right now, she's got no pulse and no heartbeat."

Moving closer, Dani zeroed in on the woman's face. Stared into her close-set, gaping eyes, almost too large for her gaunt face. Her pointy, slightly crooked nose and pinched lips. The sharp cheekbones, which were smeared with red lipstick. The longer she looked, the more familiar her face grew. And then it hit like a blow to the chest, leaving her fighting to breathe. "Is that—is that Brandy Orland?"

Officer Rose's bushy eyebrows shot up toward his creased his forehead. "It is. Do you know her?"

"I do. Brandy was a journalist who occasionally wrote for *The Maxwell Times*. She's interviewed me a few times in the past." Dani turned away, catching a glimpse of her reflection in the mirror. For a moment, she didn't recognize the shell-shocked person staring back. "The last time we spoke, I'd sung Lieutenant Edwards's praises for his mentorship."

"Oh, yeah. I remember it well. That was a really nice feature. People were buzzing about it for weeks."

Snatching a small notepad from her pocket, Dani's hand shook as she frantically scribbled her thoughts. "See, I knew the lieutenant's murder might've somehow been directed at me. And now this…this one looks like it is, too. I think somebody's trying to send me a message."

Dani pivoted toward Von, flinching at the sight of sweat beading across his forehead. When he blew a trembling breath and loosened his tie, she asked, "What's going on with you?"

"Nothing. Well, not nothing…something just hit me. This town has another dead body on its hands. I'm starting to wonder if this is a targeted attack on RPS."

"Wait, why would you think that?"

"For starters, both of these recent murders occurred on my company's watch. That makes RPS look pretty damn incompetent. Who would want to hire a security firm that can't protect its clients?"

"You make a good point. But I don't think this is about you," Dani insisted, her bun coming undone as she shook her head emphatically. "This is about the Maxwell PD. More specifically, it's about me."

"How is that?"

"Didn't you hear what I just told Officer Rose?"

"No, I missed it. What did you—"

"Chief Miller!" Officer Rose cut in. "Can you come and take a look at this?"

"I'll be right there!" Dani's words tumbled out in a rush as her eyes remained fixed on Von. "I think you're way off base. And I don't know what else to tell you. But I do need to get to work—"

"We need to talk," he interrupted, his voice dropping almost to a whisper. "In private. Because I think *you're* way off base, and I need to set you straight—especially if you still believe that RPS has anything to do with this. Once we're done here, why don't we go and grab a coffee? Somewhere discreet, where no one will see us."

Dani hesitated. Meeting with Von privately felt like a betrayal to her father. And to the Maxwell PD. But if he held information that could help solve the case, ignoring him would be a betrayal to the entire town.

"Fine," she relented. "Let's meet up at Red Mesa Café. It's open twenty-four hours."

"Red Mesa Café…isn't that about forty-five minutes away, near the border of Sagebrush Valley?"

"It is. Didn't you suggest we meet somewhere discreet? It doesn't get much more inconspicuous than that dive."

"True. All right then. I'll see you there."

A CLOUD OF DUST billowed around Dani's sedan as she turned into the café's parking lot. Von was already there, sitting inside his car while typing away on his cell phone. He appeared startled when she pulled in beside him, his wide-eyed shock quickly melting into a sheepish grin.

"Sorry I scared you!" she called out through the passenger window.

"Scared is a bit of a stretch. More like surprised, that's all."

"Yeah, okay, tough guy."

Dani stepped out of the car, her feet tingling with surreality as she and Von walked toward the entrance. It still hadn't quite sunken in that she and her lifelong nemesis had set aside their differences—at least temporarily. When it came to the safety of her hometown, the provisional truce was well worth it.

Keep your guard up, Dani reminded herself, still not fully convinced of RPS's innocence.

"This place has certainly seen better days," she said, glancing up at the café's shabby wooden exterior. The peeling blue paint had succumbed to the desert's harsh sun and shifting sands. The signage, now tattered and frayed, had been worn down to a meager *Re esa Caf.*

"Yeah, but if the coffee is hot and the pound cake is fresh, then it'll do," Von replied, giving her a slight smile while holding open the frosted glass door. "After you."

"Thank you," Dani murmured, ignoring the shiver that raced up her arm when she slid past him. Decent terms aside, there was no way in hell she could be feeling any sort of attraction toward the man she'd hated for years. Yet if he was attempting to put her at ease after a difficult night, it was working.

She stepped inside, almost losing her footing on the uneven black-and-white linoleum tile. The café's interior may have been worse than the exterior. Old, scuffed-up wooden tables and chairs were scattered about haphazardly. Grungy booths lining the walls were riddled with cracked blue cushions. A few sleepy patrons were seated at a counter cluttered with tattered menus and scuffed dishware. But there was no ignoring the rich, roasted scent of freshly brewed coffee, which was what Dani needed the most.

"Good evening, folks!" a pudgy older woman called out from behind the counter. "Take a seat wherever you'd like. I'll be with you in a sec. Can I start you off with a couple of coffees?"

"That would be great, thanks," Von said before leading Dani toward a booth in the back. Once seated, he gave her hand a gentle nudge. "So, Danielle Sabrina Miller. Who would've thought that you and I would one day be sitting across from each other like this…"

"Without clawing each other's eyes out? I know, right? But wait, how do you know my middle name?"

"I know a lot about you. More than you probably realize…"

Von's eyes lingered on her perplexed expression a beat too long, only breaking when the server approached with their coffee.

"Do you two need to see a menu?" she asked, her wide grin putting her gapped teeth on full display. "And before you answer, let me just tell you that we're out of fried catfish and Italian sausages. But we've still got plenty of burgers and beef stew."

The thought of ingesting a heavy meal after leaving the crime scene churned Dani's stomach. As she struggled to shake off the lingering unease, Von replied, "I think we're good on food. Maybe just a couple of slices of pound cake if there's any left?"

"I just put a fresh one in the oven. I'll bring over a couple of slices as soon as it's done. Be back soon."

Rubbing his hands together, Von sat back, his head tilting curiously. "Back to our convo. Aside from this investigation, you and I have a lot to catch up on, don't we?"

"Not that I'm aware of. We came here to talk about this case. Not to catch up on old times. Or did I miss the memo?"

Her prickly response seemed to amuse Von as his lips spread into a charming smirk. "Come on, Chief. Don't do me like that. I'm just trying to break the ice here before we get into all the heavy stuff."

His words disarmed her. Put her at ease. She met his intense gaze. It was the same piercing look he'd given her that night at the Zonian, before the attack. But now she saw it in a different light. Behind his eyes, there was quiet sincerity. A softness that make him seem genuine and caring. And dare she say, appealing…

"Fine," Dani blurted. "You're right. We do have a lot to catch up on. A lifetime's worth, if you really think about it. But um…" Her voice drifted as she thought back on Von's panicked reaction at the crime scene. Nothing about it seemed forced, as if he had any involvement. "I should probably start by apologizing to you for my behavior. Particularly how I treated you that night at the grocery store. I was rude, and accusatory, and blamed you for things without any proof. And I, um… I hope you'll accept my apology."

Von straightened, his body leaning in toward the table as his smirk slowly melted into a full-bodied grin. "Wow, Chief Miller. Thank you for that. I really appreciate the apology, and of course I accept it. Believe it or not, I do understand where your defensiveness comes from. You've been hit with a lot. And now, with a fresh pair of murders on your hands, the threats against you…all that would set anybody off."

"Well I appreciate your understanding. And you're right. Things really have been tough. Not to mention confusing. I can't seem to wrap my mind around why someone would be targeting me."

"Maybe that's because these murders aren't about you."

"Here we go," Dani uttered, her lips twisting with doubt. She grabbed the creamer dispenser and banged against the side until clumpy white powder poured into her cup. "How could they not be when I'm so closely tied to both victims?"

"I don't know. You're the chief of police. In some ways, you're tied to practically everybody in this town! So it could just be a coincidence. But again, you know what isn't? The fact that both murders occurred on RPS's watch. I know I've got a few enemies out here. I could name several of your officers who aren't particularly fond of me. And you already know why. It's all about the power struggle between our respective agencies."

"Well, maybe your guys need to take responsibility for their part in that. The Maxwell PD has dealt with a lot of RPS hate. We don't have to get too deep into it. But our shared history is toxic. If we're being honest, most of that negativity was coming from *your* side of the fence. Not mine. My department's success in solving cases triggered RPS's need to overstep their bounds. That didn't sit well with the force."

Von snatched a wad of napkins from the holder and pressed them against his forehead. "Let me ask you this. Did you notice any of that behavior coming directly from me?"

"It doesn't matter. It came from your employees. They're a direct reflection of you."

"Point taken. And now that you've said that, I'll have a talk with my employees. Tell them to stand down and—" He stopped mid-sentence, staring up at the wall while tapping his fingertips against the table.

"What's happening right now?" Dani asked. "What are you doing?"

"I'm thinking. And I've got an idea. But I don't know if you'd be down with it."

"I'm listening."

"What if we put something together for our agencies? Like some sort of joint event? We could do it someplace neutral, like the Zonian. What do you think?"

Dani shifted in her seat, careful not to rip her black slacks on the torn cushion.

"That's um, that's interesting. Actually, it's a pretty good idea. But the question is, will my officers agree?"

"There's only one way to find out."

The pair paused when their server approached with two slices of pound cake. "Enjoy, folks!"

"Thank you," Von said, immediately digging in as soon as his plate hit the table.

When Dani failed to pick up her fork, he asked, "Aren't you going to have any?"

"I will. I'm still coming down off that scene at the hotel."

"Understood. So, with everything that's going on, how are you holding up? I know you're well protected since you've got the entire force looking out for you. But, emotionally. How are you doing?"

Cutting into her cake, Dani slid a small bite onto her fork. "For starters, being on the force doesn't give me an automatic sense of safety. It literally feels like I could be under attack at any given moment. There's an anxious feeling of vulnerability that comes with the job. But with that being said, I'm holding it together."

"Is there anything I can do to help? Like keep watch over your house, or provide you with personal security detail? Free of charge, of course."

"You know, as cool as it would be to go all Whitney Houston à la *The Bodyguard*, I think I'm good. I do appreciate the offer, though. It's interesting, you offering to protect me after I was convinced you were behind all this."

"Man, I *still* haven't gotten over the way you went off on me at Cole's."

Dani's embarrassment turned into a fit of wheezing coughs. "Yeah, I, um… I'm sorry about that, too. And not that I'm trying to run up a list of excuses or anything, but I was under a ton of stress that day."

"I know you were. But I'm not gonna let you off the hook that easily. Seriously, you went *in.* I mean, you talked about my father—"

"I know! I know. I shouldn't have gone there. It's crazy how after all this time, you and I never discussed the beef between our dads. I'm sure the stories you've heard are much different from the ones I've gotten."

"Oh, I bet they are." Von rested against the back of the booth and folded his arms over his brawny chest. "Since you bring it up, I'm curious. What did your father tell you about their rivalry?"

Dani was slow to respond, her eyes lingering on the outline of his biceps, bulging through his crisp white shirt. The way his rolled-up sleeves exposed his muscular forearms…

What in the hell are you doing?

She focused her attention on the space above Von's head to avoid looking directly at him. "Well, here's something you may not know. My father always thought that your dad saw his promotion to police chief as a result of favoritism, not merit, since he was close with a lot of Maxwell's movers and shakers. Plus your dad struggled with the idea of having a friend as his boss."

Von let off a condescending chuckle, then scarfed down a mouthful of cake, as if to avoid saying the wrong thing.

"I'm guessing your version of the story is different," Dani said.

"Yes, way different. The thing is, our fathers were both competitive. My dad always believed he was the best man for the job, but never doubted your dad deserved it. In the end, my father thought Mr. Miller was too tough on him. Because they were friends, maybe your dad pushed too hard to prove he wouldn't show favoritism. Either way, it didn't sit well with my father, and he felt he had to leave."

"Hmm, okay. They certainly did have two totally different perspectives. But it sounds like there were quite a few misunderstandings between them that could've been worked out had they just taken the time to sit down and talk."

"I agree," Von said. "But instead they let their emotions get the best of them and jumped to a lot of conclusions. Little did they know their personal feud would trigger enough fury to affect the entire town."

"To the point where it would last for decades."

"Yeah, well, us sitting down and talking like two mature adults is a move in the right direction. It could actually be the catalyst that'll turn this situation around."

Dani nodded, surprised by the weight of relief brought on by his words. She hadn't realized how heavy the burden of their rivalry had become.

"Look," Von continued after scraping his plate clean, "if nothing else, I'm just glad that you finally came to your senses and realized that I'm not some psychopath."

"Yeah, *you're* not, but..."

"But what?"

"You might be off the hook, but I'm still not sure about all of RPS."

"Chief Miller, are you serious? Do you really think that

one of my employees, each of whom I thoroughly vetted, is a killer?"

"At this point, I'm not putting anything past anybody." *Including my own officers*, she thought but kept to herself. Dani wasn't ready to admit that truth to Von.

"Fair point. But as for me, I will continue to vouch for all of my employees until the evidence says otherwise. Speaking of which, how long do you think it'll take the lab to send back the results from tonight's crime scene?"

"We're expecting to hear something within the next two weeks. The forensics investigator requested that they put a rush on it. Hopefully we'll have more luck with this one than the one at Cole's."

Sliding his coffee stirrer between his lips, Von said, "I'd been wondering about that. So nothing came of the evidence you collected at the lieutenant's crime scene?"

Dani's gaze fell to her half-eaten piece of cake. There was no way she could respond while watching his full, inviting lips curl around that straw. "Nope. Nothing. The resort doesn't have cameras installed inside the stairwells, so that wasn't helpful. The footage from nearby areas didn't offer any answers either. We did have a promising lead involving one of Lieutenant Edwards's sons. But his alibi checked out. CCTV footage confirmed that he and a friend were in California at the time of the murder."

"What about the maintenance guy who discovered the body? I think his name is Mr. Stallworth?"

"Yes, that's him. He wasn't able to provide us with much information. Some of my officers thought he could be our suspect. But witnesses saw him inside the employee cafeteria at the time of the murder, so he was cleared."

"Got it..." Von grew quiet, running his fingertip along a chip in his mug. "I know this is none of my business, but when it comes to this case, I've been so curious as to what's happening on the inside. It seems that this go-round, Maxwell PD is being pretty tight-lipped with the media and what information you're releasing to the public."

"We are. And that's because we don't want to say anything that might compromise the investigation. Our suspect may alter his behavior, destroy evidence or fabricate his story once he's brought in for questioning. Plus we don't wanna scare away potential witnesses who may fear we'd put them at risk by revealing more than necessary. So to avoid those types of pitfalls, we just remain quiet and hope that the evidence will speak for itself."

"Got it." The furrows etched into Von's forehead softened, giving way to a subtle hint of worry. "I hate to bring this up, Chief, but um…your vehicle being vandalized that night at the grocery store. Whatever came of it?"

"Ugh," she groaned, shoving a large chunk of cake in her mouth out of frustration.

"Just breathe," Von murmured, covering his mouth as if to stifle a laugh. "And please don't choke."

"What, you think this is funny?"

"No! Of course not. I'm just not used to seeing you going in on a piece of cake like that. It's actually kind of cute."

"Anyway," Dani said, ignoring the flirtatious glimmer in his eyes, "my Jeep is at the crime lab being processed now, so hopefully they'll recover some sort of evidence. As for the security footage from that night, all I saw was a figure dressed in dark, bulky clothing, hovering around my vehicle. He was wearing a baseball cap, a hoodie and large sunglasses that almost covered his entire face. That was pretty terrifying, watching him destroy my car like that. Especially since there was nothing I could do about it. I couldn't even get a good look at the person. But when I think about Lieutenant Edwards and Brandy Orland, I realize things could've been much worse."

"Oh, absolutely. What's clear to me is that you've got a brazen murderer on your hands who's killing on a grand scale. It's pretty shocking how bold these crimes have been."

"And what's clear to me is that we're dealing with someone who's pretty damn audacious. Someone who won't stop killing until we stop him. In the meantime, the entire force is on high alert. My house is under twenty-four-hour surveillance, seven days a week. My security system is on whether I'm home or not. Troy and Chloe barely want to leave my side. At this point, it feels like I'm in a witness protection program."

"Which isn't a bad thing…"

As Von's hand inched across the table toward her, Dani snatched her phone and checked the time. "Ooh, I didn't realize it had gotten so late. I need to get home."

"Yeah, I uh… I guess should get going, too. Thanks for agreeing to meet with me. This was good. Really good. A step in the right direction, if you will. And just so you know, if there's anything I can do to help, say the word. I may not be a part of the Maxwell PD, but I wouldn't mind stepping in to assist. So let me know. I'd be happy to slide into the rotation."

"I will do that. Thank you."

The gaze shared between them lingered, stretching several beats longer than necessary. Dani was the first to break, staring down at the bits of creamer floating inside her mug. Her skin burned underneath Von's unwavering stare. The intensity stirred emotions buried deep within her tough exterior, leaving her fingers fidgeting and stomach fluttering.

Please look away, her inner voice pleased. But he didn't. She refused to make eye contact for fear of what might spark within her.

The spell broke when the server walked over and placed

the check on the table. After paying the bill, Von stood. "You ready?"

"I am." A sense of calm fell over Dani as she followed him toward the exit. "And I'm glad we did this. Next time we see each other, hopefully it'll be under better circumstances. Like me telling you that we've arrested the killer. Wouldn't that be nice?"

"Yes, it would be. Because honestly? I don't think this town can handle a repeat of last year."

Chapter Nine

The Maxwell PD's joint social with RPS was in full swing. Dani was pleasantly surprised by the turnout since it was her and Von's first attempt to mend the rift between their agencies. The Zonian was packed, with everyone clearly enjoying themselves as drinks flowed freely, games of pool were in motion, and the room vibrated with R&B hits.

But while the walls were lined with employees from both organizations, the bar felt divided. The police department dominated the right side of the room, and RPS occupied the left. No one was mingling across the divide.

Dani and Von were holding court in the middle of the floor, hoping their friendly interaction would inspire others to follow suit. So far, it hadn't. Troy was doing his best to break the ice, chatting with a few of the RPS officers. Yet no one seemed willing to take his cue, either.

"We need to do something to loosen things up around here," Dani said to Von. "Something that'll get our teams out of their little cliques. Maybe we should play one of the games we discussed."

"Good idea. Because at the rate they're going, we'll be here all night without making any progress."

"Which one should we start with? Two Truths and a Lie, Would You Rather, or Human Bingo?"

"I think Two Truths and a Lie would be a good one," Von

said. "That way we can all learn a little something about each other. And I'm sure the stuff they'll come up with will drum up some laughs. Humor is always a great way to cut through the awkwardness."

"Good point. All right, let's do it."

Dani led him to the DJ booth and grabbed hold of the mic.

"Hey, party people!" she exclaimed, her voice booming over the raucous crowd. "Can I please get your attention? First of all, Von and I would like to extend a heartfelt thank you to everyone who came out tonight. We really appreciate each of you for accepting our invitation, and acknowledging our effort to mend fences between the Maxwell PD and Reed Protective Services. I'm sure you all realize this, but please allow me to reiterate the fact that our agencies are two of the most important organizations in this town. And while our history may be somewhat...*contentious*—"

"To put it mildly," Von cut in, drawing a laugh from the crowd.

"Exactly," Dani continued with an amused eye roll. "But that's why we're here tonight. To start a conversation, heal the rift, and move forward in a more positive way. This room is filled with so many passionate, highly trained officers who all have one thing in common—our love of Maxwell. So instead of just talking about it, let's actually be about it, starting with being a little kinder toward one another. You think we can we do that?"

A wave of hushed mutters swept through the room.

"Really?" Dani continued. "Now I hate to be the one who gets on the mic and says things like, *you can do better than that*, but people, I *know* you can do better than that. So again I ask, are you willing to show a little more love toward one another?"

Pulling the mic toward him, Von threw in, "Or at least a little more *like*?"

The crowd responded more enthusiastically this time, with cheers erupting and glasses raised high.

"All right then," Dani said through a satisfied smile. "That's more like it! Now I'm gonna turn the mic over to my cohost, Von Reed, who's going to share the deets on the icebreaking game we'll be playing."

"Thank you, Chief Miller. What's up, everybody? Just to echo the chief's gratitude, thanks again for coming out. And before I start, let's all give her a round of applause. While my name is on the bill, she pretty much planned this entire night on her own."

A thunderous roar shook the floor. Dani clutched her hands to her chest, mouthing the words *thank you* as Von quieted the crowd. There was something undeniably appealing about the way he stood there, confident and composed, commanding the room in his cool blue linen suit and fitted white T-shirt.

Coincidentally, she'd opted for blue as well. Her ombré bodycon midi dress went from powdery to sky to a deep shade of teal. She'd straightened her hair and applied smoky eye-shadow with a deep peach gloss. The look was sexier than normal, proven by her team's speechless reaction when she'd walked through the door. But no one's was as blatant as Von's. He hadn't taken his eyes off of her since he'd arrived.

"So listen up, everyone," Von continued. "We're gonna kick the night off with a game called Two Truths and a Lie. The way it works is that each person who's called to the DJ booth will share two true statements about themselves, and one false statement. The rest of us will have to guess what's factual and what isn't. Now since this is just for fun, there won't be much order in how it goes down. We'll just shout out what we're thinking, see what the majority says, then have whoever's up to the mic give us the correct response. Got it?"

"Got it!" the crowd declared in unison.

It was the most enthusiastic reaction they'd gotten all night. Dani noticed the two agencies slowly merging as they moved to the middle of the floor. Several of them had even begun chatting with one another.

"It's already working," she whispered in Von's ear.

"Yeah, I see. Good job," he said, giving her a high five. "So do you wanna kick the game off, or should I do the honors?"

"Please, you do the honors. You're doing great. Everybody seems to be enjoying your commentary. Even my team."

"Thanks for the reassurance." Von punctuated his gratitude with a wink, then said to the crowd, "Let's get started! Go ahead and pull out the numbers you were given when you arrived. Numbers one through ten, we're gonna start with you. We'll give you a few minutes to come up with two truths and a lie. After that, line up next to Dani and me, then we'll go from there."

"Don't forget to tell them about the prize," Dani whispered in his ear.

"Oh, listen up! The winner of each game will receive a gift card to the lovely Canyon Catch seafood restaurant. So get loud, get rowdy, let your voice be heard, and most importantly, have fun. Good luck!"

Von handed the mic back to the DJ, who turned up the music. The crowd began bobbing their heads to Tinashe's "Nasty" while several guests made their way toward the booth.

"You know what?" Dani said. "I know it's still early, but I think it's safe to say that this event is a success."

"I think so, too. But let's not speak too soon and jinx it. The night is young. Anything can happen."

"True. However, I'm gonna err on the side of positivity and declare it a good night."

"You know what would make it an even better night?" Von asked.

"What's that?"

"If you'd dance with me."

Dani's heart rate sped up, thumping to the beat of the music as Von pulled her close. His arms circled her waist. Swaying gradually, his hips moved in a slow, provocative rhythm. She slid her hands onto his shoulders. Relaxed as her body fell in sync with his. When she sang along to Tinashe's hook, Von released a low moan, the warmth of his breath gently caressing her skin.

"Oh, so you've been a nasty girl, huh?" he quipped.

As Von spoke, his lips brushed against her neck. His touch sent a trail of quivers straight through her.

"Excuse me, Mr. Reed, but are you flirting with me?"

"Maybe. Would it be a bad thing if I am?"

"I don't know yet. But right now, considering where we are? You'd better cut it out."

"Are you sure about that?" Von debated. "Because I didn't hear an ounce of conviction in your voice. You're gonna have to come stronger than that if you really want me to stop."

"Hey, Reed!" someone called out from the DJ booth. "What's up? Are you gonna get this game going or what?"

Von tossed him a thumbs-up, then slowly pulled away from Dani. It took everything in her to release him from her embrace.

Whatever the hell this is you're doing, stop it!

As he stepped back to the mic, his gaze remained on her. "You still owe me the rest of that dance. So make sure you don't leave here tonight without settling your debt."

"Trust me, I won't."

The response was out of her mouth before she'd thought it through. But it was too late to take it back. When Von licked his lips, Dani questioned whether or not she even wanted to.

Taking her hand in his, Von positioned her next to him. An awkward grin crept across her face. She scanned the room. Checked to see if anyone was watching them. Then locked eyes with Troy and Chloe. They were staring back at her, wearing matching expressions of disbelief.

Dani ignored them, making a mental note to explain whatever was happening between her and Von later. Or at least attempt to, given she didn't fully understand it herself.

"Party people," Von sang into the mic. "Let's get things under way. First up, we've got my guy, Kevin Freelain. For those of you who don't know, Kevin is the vice president of RPS. He's also my right-hand man who helps keep the company running smoothly. Kev, I'm turning the mic over to you. Give us your two truths and a lie. And no pressure, but they'd better be good since you're this jumping this game off and repping my company."

Kevin's head rolled back before he replied, "Oh, no pressure, huh?"

"You got this, Kev!" someone yelled out, prompting everyone else to whoop and whistle in support.

"Thanks, guys. All right, here we go. Three things about me. Number one. I've never read a full book."

"Truth!" several people shouted in unison.

When a wave of laughter flooded the bar, Dani leaned into Von. "So far so good on the game."

"Of course. You were the one who came up with it."

"Well you were the one who come up with the idea to throw this event. So thank you. I really do think it's gonna help quash the beef between our agencies."

"I think so, too. Plus," Von said, "this night gives us a chance to spend some time together."

His fingertips brushed against her palm, sending a wave of tingles to places she hadn't tingled in months. Dani couldn't decide if it was the gin and tonic fueling Von's boldness, or if he was genuinely drawn to her. Either way, the struggle to catch her breath proved the feelings may be mutual.

"As for my second truth or lie," Kevin continued, "I graduated college summa cum laude."

"Now we *know* that's a lie!" Officer Bryant hollered.

"You'd better watch yourself, B," Kevin retorted. "Don't mess around and let this game get you fired. Anyway, last but not least, number three. I have never been drunk."

"You're drunk right now!" Bryant shot back, ignoring the warning.

Boisterous laughter rocked the bar as the DJ dropped a beat. After giving Kevin an enthusiastic high five, Von took over the mic.

"Good job, man. Okay everybody, on the count of three, tell me which statement you think is a lie. Is Kevin stretching the truth about being a nonreader, a genius or a lightweight drinker? One, two, three!"

The crowd's loud rumbling was hard to make out. Dani and Von held their hands to their ears, urging everyone to yell louder.

"Is it me?" Von asked, "or am I hearing everyone say they think Kevin is lying about being a lightweight drinker?"

Taking over the mic, Dani replied, "I think you're right. The majority of our guests seem to think that Kevin is lying about never being drunk. So now it's your turn, Kev. Tell us, which is the lie?"

"The lie is, drumroll please…that I've never been drunk!"

The response incited a reaction so raucous that Dani had to cover her ears.

"Great job, everybody!" Von said. "Kevin, I'm gonna let you choose your winner, then take over the game while the lady of the hour and I take a quick break. Good luck!"

Taking Dani's hand once again, Von led her toward a secluded corner near the back of the bar. On the way there, she peered straight ahead, dodging the inquisitive stares of their guests while forcing a strained smile. Their shock was understandable. For years, the town had witnessed the volatile dynamics of Dani and Von's contentious relationship. Just a matter of days ago, Dani had added him to the list of suspects. Now here she was, not only tolerating his presence, but feeling a strange magnetic pull toward him—one that she couldn't quite explain or ignore.

"This hosting gig is exhausting, isn't it?" Von asked after they'd found two empty stools.

"Absolutely. It's fun, but it's definitely tiring. When you think about everything it took to put this night together, it's fair to say we're both worn out."

"Agreed. And since we've got such capable folks working for our agencies, I'm fine letting them take over for a bit while we cool out. Now, what are you drinking?" Von asked while flagging down the bartender.

"I'd love a mojito. Thanks."

After being served another round, Von held his glass to hers. "To us. For planning a fantastic event that brought both our teams together, and burying the hatchet. Hopefully for good. Cheers."

"Cheers to that." Dani took a leisurely sip, allowing the tangy fizz to settle on her tongue before swallowing it down.

Just as she went for another, Von asked, "So…are you seeing anybody these days?"

The question turned her sip into a gulp, which sent a mint leaf sliding down her throat. A coughing fit prompted Von to leap from his stool and massage her back until her breathing normalized.

"Are you okay?" he asked.

"I—I'm fine. Your question just took me by surprise. That's all."

"Really? I'm sorry. I didn't think I was being intrusive—"

"No, it isn't that. I'm just not used to us being this cordial and open with each other. Don't get me wrong. I'm actually enjoying it. But it's all so strange. You and I have spent our entire lives hating each other. So it's an adjustment."

"For sure. However, we agreed to turn all that around, starting with tonight. So get used to this. Also, stop trying to dodge my question. Spill it. What's going on with your love life?"

Dani's head tilted curiously as she studied his expression. The raised brows and parted lips indicated that he was truly clueless. But she was almost certain Von knew she was single.

"To put it simply," she said, "there isn't much going on with my love life. I'm not seeing anyone."

"Hmm, okay. Interesting…"

Dani could've sworn she saw a spark of satisfaction flicker across Von's eyes. He nodded, running the rim of his glass along his lips before taking a long, deliberate sip. Her gaze fell to his tongue. A piece of ice slid inside his mouth. He sucked it, slowly, his soft lips forming a pout as the cube rolled from side to side.

What are you trying to do to me? she fought the urge to blurt while pressing her thighs together.

"So um…are you seeing anyone?" she asked.

"Not at the moment, no."

"Are you sure? Because according to the streets, you're pretty popular out here on the dating scene."

"Is that what they're saying? Where in the world did you hear that?"

Spinning in her stool, Dani turned her back to Von while laughing hysterically. "Oh, *please.* Are you seriously asking me that? All of Maxwell is aware of your reputation for being a playboy. And from what I know personally, it's well earned."

"Is that what you know personally, or is that what you *heard*?"

"Look, there's no need to go back and forth on this. We both know the truth. So just answer the question!"

"I already did!" Von insisted. "The answer was no a few seconds ago, and it's still no. Now whether or not you choose to believe me, that's on you."

"Okay, that's fair. All I can do is take your word for it. But I do know you've got a pretty active dating life. Correction. That's what I've *heard.* Anyway, tell me. When was your last relationship?"

"Humph, let me think..." his gaze drifted as his expression slipped into a deep, thoughtful daze. "Honestly, I haven't been in a serious relationship for a while now. I've just dated casually here and there."

"And why didn't those situations turn into anything serious?"

The question was out before she knew it. Dani cringed, confused as to why she was suddenly so curious about Von's love life.

You know why. So stop while you're ahead...

"Since I've taken over RPS, I haven't really had time to even think about settling down. But I do take pleasure in the company of women. So when I connect with someone, I make it clear that I'm not looking for a commitment."

"Ahh, not looking for a commitment. Those are words that most women aren't looking to hear."

"They are. However, most women never admit to that. They'll oftentimes claim it's cool and they're not looking for anything serious either. Then after a little time passes, suddenly they change their tune. I'll give you an example. A few months ago, I met a woman from Scottsdale at the Singalong Karaoke Bar. Her name was Jessica. She came to town often to visit her sister. During our very first phone conversation, I told her I wasn't looking for a commitment. According to Jessica, she wasn't either. So we started hanging out, and I tried to keep things casual. But she latched on pretty quickly and even starting talking about moving to Maxwell so we could be closer to each other. After that, I started to back off. But the more I faded, the harder she went. At one point, she even suggested that we move in together, and started dropping hints about marriage."

"Wait, and you two had been dating for how long at that point?"

Holding two fingers in the air, Von replied, "A couple of months. But after that, I had to cut things off. And I did so gently, reminding her that I'd been honest about my intentions from the beginning. She was a little salty for a while, and dropped a few angry texts and voicemails. But eventually, she got over it and moved on. After that, I met a woman named…" He hesitated, a self-deprecating smirk crinkling his eyes.

"Wait, why'd you stop?"

"Because you didn't ask me to run down my entire dating résumé."

Dani took another sip of her mojito, allowing the rum to dissolve her inhibitions. Sliding her stool closer to his, she murmured, "No, please. Go on. This conversation is getting interesting."

"Okay, as long as you're not judging me."

"I listen and I don't judge," she insisted, her thigh brushing against his.

"Cool," he rasped, resting his hand on her knee. "I appreciate that about you. So anyway, after Jessica, I met a woman named Melody. There's not much to say about her. She was a little too young and way too wild for me. That situation didn't last long at all. And then..." Von paused, covering a smirk with his glass before taking a hefty sip.

"What's with the sly grin?" Dani asked.

"I'm kind of embarrassed to tell you about my most recent dating adventure. Because you may very well judge me on this one."

"Uh-oh. Who was she?"

"Carmen Pendleton."

"Carmen Pendleton," Dani squealed, clutching Von's arm. "As in our former high school classmate?"

"Yes. Her. I don't know if you remember this, but her dad used to work for RPS. He'd just left the navy and was one of the first officers my father hired back when the company first launched. So Carmen and I actually go way back."

"Ooh, okay. I didn't see that one coming. I never would've pegged her as your type. I mean, she's attractive and all, but Carmen was always so vapid and self-centered. Didn't she move to LA to pursue an acting career at some point?"

"She did. And she landed a few minor film roles, too. I actually saw her in one of them. *The Last Breath Before Midnight*, or something like that. It was a pretty cheesy thriller."

"Carmen moved back to Maxwell, didn't she?"

"She did. When she left for LA, I think she expected to book a ton of A-list roles the minute her plane landed. When that didn't happen, she moved back home. We went out a couple of times, but all she talked about was herself, her acting career, and how she was dying to get back to LA. This town isn't enough for her. It never has been. Those two dates told me all I needed to know. We weren't a good match."

He was cut off when a series of air horns blasted through the speakers.

"Von Reed!" Kevin shouted into the mic. "Your presence, along with Chief Miller's, is needed at the DJ booth."

"Welp, I guess our little break is over," Von said.

"I guess it is. This was nice. Thanks for sharing with me. And for admitting how you've been breaking women's hearts all over town."

"Why would you lie on me to my face like that?" he joked, taking Dani's hand and helping her up. "I may be a lot of things, but a heartbreaker isn't one of them."

Wrapping an arm around her, Von led the way toward the front of the bar. This time, she didn't avoid the crowd's probing stares. She was, however, taken aback when his fingertips caressed her shoulder, then slid up her neck.

When they reached the booth, their eyes locked. The air between them felt charged. Dani could sense herself slipping, succumbing to their burgeoning attraction. While Von's jovial smile and easy demeanor seemed friendly enough, the heat in his touch was far from platonic. Her mind spun with possibilities as she wondered what this all meant, and where things may go. But the biggest thrill was the uncertainty of how their night would end.

Chapter Ten

"Von," Dani said as he followed her up the driveway toward her quaint bungalow. "I know you're tired. You really didn't have to follow me home. And you certainly don't have to walk me to my door. I told you, I'm fine."

He didn't respond immediately, instead staring up at her house. He'd driven past it countless times. But he had never been this close. Von studied the soft beige stucco walls, olive wooden shutters, and winding cobblestoned walkway leading to a charming arched door. Clusters of vibrant succulents lined a tiered rock garden. The warmth of it all enveloped him, driving an urge to step inside.

"I know you're fine," he said. "But I wouldn't have been okay letting you drive home alone."

"Letting me?" Dani asked with a smirk.

"You know what I meant."

"I do. And I appreciate it. However, you seem to have forgotten that I'm a police chief. Who's armed at all times."

"Were you a police chief when someone attacked you that night you left the Zonian alone? Or when your Jeep was vandalized outside of the grocery store? How about when those threatening messages—"

"Okay, okay," she interrupted, pressing her hand against Von's chest to silence him. "I get it. And again, I appreciate you." She spun around on her heels and dug inside her clutch. “I can’t see a thing. I forgot to turn the porch light on before I left.”

“Here, this should help.” He pulled out his cell and shone the flashlight near her purse. The jingle of her keys soon followed.

“Thank you,” Dani murmured, moving toward the door so suddenly that she nearly stumbled into him.

Grabbing her waist, Von pulled her upright, his body stiffening as she clung to him. “Whoa, you good?”

“Yep,” she uttered, her embarrassment clear as she steadied herself. “I’m good. I didn’t realize you were standing so close.”

“Sorry about that. I didn’t mean to startle you…” His voice drifted when he glanced down the block. “So the officer who’s supposed to be keeping an eye on your house tonight called in sick?”

“He did.”

“See, it was meant for me to be here tonight.”

The buzz of Dani’s phone cut into the moment.

“I already know that’s Troy,” she said. “He’s probably checking to make sure I made it home.”

“Tell him that you’re fine. And that he doesn’t have to worry about you tonight. I’ve got you.”

“I’m sure hearing that is going to freak him out.”

“Why would it?” Von asked.

“Um, I’m sorry, but have you forgotten that we’ve been sworn enemies? Finding out that you and I are suddenly cool would freak anybody out.”

“Well, it shouldn’t. Especially not Troy. I’m sure he saw us hanging out tonight and picked up on the good vibes.”

“Probably so…” she agreed while typing away on her phone. “Thanks again for following me home. Feel free to get going. You’ve been at it nonstop all day, and I know you’re ready to call it a night. I can take it from here.”

"*No...* I'm gonna stand here and make sure you get inside safely. Lock the door behind you. Turn on the lights. And wave goodbye through the door."

Dani tucked the phone back inside her purse and stared up at Von. As silence fell over the pair, he noticed a sultriness in her gaze that he'd never seen before.

"You don't have to rush home if you're not ready," she said, her voice dropping to a soft whisper.

Stepping in closer, Von wrapped his arm around her waist. "What exactly are you saying, Chief Miller?"

"What I'm saying is, you can come inside if you want. Maybe have a nightcap. Debrief over tonight's event. That is unless you've got plans with Melody, or Jessica, or Carmen, or—"

"Okay, you can stop right there. I don't have any plans with anybody. And I'd love to come in and rehash our evening over a nightcap."

"Cool. Follow me."

When Dani cracked opened the door, a warm rush of air brushed against Von's skin. He entered after her, inhaling the sweet scent of lemon and vanilla. The dim interior slowly came into focus, illuminated by the warm glow of chrome lights suspended from the vaulted ceiling. Not surprising, the spacious living room was in perfect order. Everything was well appointed, with a touch of Dani's chic style spread throughout.

The swanky cream-colored furniture was lined with plush lilac throw pillows. A vintage leather coffee table was stacked with statement books and a crystal chess set. Floating shelves made of reclaimed wood were filled with an eclectic selection of novels, service awards and decorative knickknacks.

Stepping into Dani's world felt surreal, beyond just entering her space. Her carefully curated home gave him a deeper understanding of who she really was. Every thoughtful detail revealed a part of her that drew him in, bringing an unexpected sense of calm and intimacy. In that moment, Von felt as though he was exactly where he belonged.

"Have a seat," she said, kicking off her nude patent heels and heading to the kitchen. "Make yourself comfortable while I grab a bottle of wine."

Von sauntered toward the couch, his eyes fixated on the sway of Dani's hips. The pull in his groin heightened at the sight of her curves swinging from right to left, as if she were putting on a show for him. Rather than take a seat, he followed her past the dining area and into the kitchen.

"How does cabernet sound?" Dani asked.

"That sounds good, thanks."

His mind spun with thoughts of the private moments they'd shared earlier that night. The time they spent away from the crowd, stealing discreet touches while swapping personal stories. The drinks and sensual dances. Von never imagined he'd get so close to Dani, let alone step inside her home. Yet here he was, reminded that life had a way of turning the impossible into something real.

"Your place is really nice," he told her. "I have to admit, I'm a little shocked you invited me in. You've hated me for so long I figured the only way I'd set foot inside of here is if you kidnapped me."

"Don't give me any ideas," Dani said with a tipsy giggle. "No, but seriously. It does feel a little odd, you being here." Handing him a glass, she added, "But it's actually nice."

"Yeah, it is. Thanks for this. For everything. May this amazing night be the first of many more to come."

"Salud," Dani murmured before taking a sip of wine.

Von was so preoccupied with her lips, still stained with a shimmery peach gloss, that he missed a question she'd just asked. His arm remained stuck midair. "I'm sorry, could you repeat that?"

"I said why don't we have a seat? And recap the night, or..."

"Talk about the investigation?"

Dani shook her head adamantly while leading him into the living room. "I'd rather *not* talk about the case. At least not tonight. If that's okay with you."

"Of course it is. As a matter of fact, why don't we shift gears altogether? Talk about us. And figure out where we should go from here."

"*We*, as in me and you?"

"No, we as in the Maxwell PD and RPS."

"Ohh," Dani muttered, biting down on her bottom lip. "Got it. Sorry for the misinterpretation."

"No need to apologize," he told her. Von wanted to add that he'd love to explore their personal connection. Find out whether it was his imagination, or if something was unfolding between them. But he didn't want to rush into that conversation or make assumptions. They'd just made amends. Pushing too soon could jeopardize the possibilities. Plus he knew she was deeply entrenched in the case. Now might not be the best time to pursue something more.

As they sank into the couch, Dani's curious gaze caught his attention. The spark in her eyes threatened to turn his unspoken thoughts into words. But he refrained, shifting his focus to the silver framed photos lining her stone fireplace mantel.

"Hey, I think I recognize some of those smiling faces up there."

"I'm sure you do. Those pictures are like a timeline of my life. You see my parents in the first one, then Troy and me, Chloe and me, Chloe and Troy..."

"And your high school crew, better known as the Classy Clique."

Dani grasped Von's arm, erupting into an infectious laugh. "Wait, I cannot believe you actually remember that! Your memory is undefeated. You've spent this entire night reminding me of stuff I've completely forgotten about."

"Yeah, well, it's pretty easy to hold on to things that mean something to you."

After her long pause, Von realized he'd said too much. He wished he could rewind time and take it back. Their sexy interactions, mixed with the alcohol, had him talking too much.

"Or," Dani began, her head tilting inquisitively, "it could just mean that names like the Classy Clique are hard to forget because they're so obnoxious. Could that be it?"

He released a subtle sigh; he sat back and unlocked his shoulders. "I actually thought the name was cute. And very fitting. You all were pretty sophisticated. But you have to admit that your crew did walk around with your noses in the air, thinking you were too good for everybody."

"That is not true! We were just in our own world, focusing on our books and goals rather than boys and partying."

"Which, in all honesty, is what made you even more appealing."

"Appealing?" Dani snorted. "*Please.* You know you couldn't stand me back then."

"Actually, it was quite the opposite. I'm just a really good actor."

"Yeah, right…"

Von's expression grew serious, his smile fading as he peered over at her. "I never disliked you, Dani. As a matter of fact, I had a huge crush on you." *Still do,* he almost let slip. "But I never acted on it because I knew better. I couldn't betray my father by trying to get together with you. Not to mention I knew you'd never go for it. You were a daddy's girl.

You wouldn't have crossed over into enemy territory and hung out with me."

"You're right about that. I actually feel a little guilty hanging out with you now. But at this point, the situation we're in—that all of Maxwell is in—is bigger than us. We can't afford to let a ridiculous beef between our fathers keep us divided. And it doesn't matter whether I'm the intended target or you are. Our best chance of catching the killer is to work together."

"Exactly. As the saying goes, there's strength in numbers."

Clinking her glass against his again, Dani replied, "That's part."

Von downed a mouthful of wine. It kept him from revisiting his earlier thoughts on whether their after-hours hangout was strictly a friend thing, or something more.

"Hey," she said softly, her fingertips gliding across his hand. "What's on your mind?"

Don't do it. Do not mess this moment up by professing your true feelings to this woman.

"I, um… I guess now that the event is over and the quiet has settled around me," Von said, "I'm back to reality. And the reality is that we do in fact have a killer on our hands. Possibly another serial killer, no less. So that's pretty deep."

"Yes, it is. But didn't we agree not to talk about the case tonight?"

"You're right," Von replied with a slow nod. "We did. So let's change the subject."

"Here's something funny that I forgot to mention—the stunned expression on Chloe's face when she saw us leaving together."

"If it was anything like Kevin's, I can already envision it."

Dani grabbed her phone and scrolled through her texts. "Those two… I felt like they were watching us all night. But Kevin seemed more irritated than shocked. Jealous even. I know that man can't stand me. Plus he's possessive and doesn't like to share you with anyone else."

"Aww, come on. Do you have to be so hard on him?"

"Just calling it like I see it. Anyway, look at this. Chloe and Troy have both sent me several messages asking whether I came home alone."

"Are you gonna tell them the truth? Or will I be your dirty little secret?"

"There is nothing dirty about this hangout."

Yet, Von's mischievous side wanted to say. But he held back.

"It's getting late," he told her. "And I've got to be at the office early tomorrow morning to process payroll. So I should probably get going."

When he set his glass down, Dani refilled it, as if she hadn't heard what he'd just said.

"You can't go yet," she told him. "I haven't answered your question."

"What question?"

"About you being my dirty little secret."

"Yes, you did. You said there's nothing dirty about us hanging out."

"Now Von," she murmured, sliding in a bit closer. "Let's be real. Is that all we're doing here? Just *hanging out*?"

The question, along with her penetrating stare, sent a surge of heat straight to his head that settled below his belt.

"I, um… I don't know," he stammered, stuck between the notion of not saying enough and saying too much. "What do you think?"

"Let's just say that there seems to be more going on than just friendly banter over drinks."

Dani always had been a tough read. But her answer was as blatant as it could get.

"I was hoping you'd say that," Von told her, unable to hold

back as his eyes roamed her body. "I think so, too. And might I add that you just opened a door I've been dying to kick down."

"Oh, have you now? I never would've guessed that."

"Well, it's the truth. But before we go any further, I have to ask you a question that you seemed to dodge while we were at the Zonian. Why are you single?"

"Oh, God," she groaned. "Are you going there?"

"Yes, I am. Look, you had no qualms grilling me over my love life. So it's only fair that I do the same to you. Plus, I'm very curious as to why a woman like you hasn't been snatched up yet."

"Hmm…well, the short answer is that I refuse to settle."

"And what's the long answer?"

Glancing down at her phone, Dani said, "You know, it really is getting late. Didn't you say you have to get up early and—"

"Don't even try it! I'm good. I don't need copious amounts of sleep in order to function. I've got plenty of time. So answer the question, please."

"I really do hate talking about this, but, since you insist… I'm single for the same reason that you are. Being the chief of police is a pretty big job. And I've dated, of course. But I date with intention. If I'm gonna take time out of my busy schedule to go out with someone, then it has to be mutually beneficial. So if I'm not getting anything out of it, or I don't see myself having a real future with him, then I'm not going to continue investing time in that person."

"Okay. I feel you on that. What about the last guy you seriously dated? Why didn't things work out with him?"

"Let's just say that he and I were complete opposites. He put on a good show in the beginning, though, convincing me that he was everything I'd been looking for in a man. Intelligent, funny, close with his family, in tune with his emotions… But he couldn't maintain the facade for long. Cracks began to form in the foundation we'd built when I realized he really wasn't ready to commit. He was still into partying with his fraternity brothers and more interested in hanging out with his friends than with me. Telling the world that I was his girlfriend was more important than actually investing in the relationship. He seemed to think that dating a law enforcement officer was a good look."

"But not good enough for him to actually put in the work?"

"Apparently not. We eventually drifted apart, and I broke things off officially when one of my girlfriends saw him on a dating app after he'd insisted we start dating exclusively. Since then, I've gone out on a few dates here and there. But nothing serious. Like I said, if I don't see a future, I don't waste my time."

"Yes, like you said, you're dating with intention," Von repeated. "I like that. Okay, here's another question. Have you ever been in love?"

Dani's head fell against the back of the couch as she stared up at the ceiling. "Ooh, that's a heavy one. I was, actually. Once. Back when I was still hopeful and carefree, believing that the world was my oyster. His name was Joshua. He was a financial analyst. We met at celebrity basketball game, and our connection was electric. We could talk for hours about anything and everything."

"Hold on, now, you're making me jealous," Von interjected, only half kidding.

"Well, you asked! But seriously, no need to be jealous since things didn't work out. Anyway, the relationship was great. I actually thought it was perfect. Then we realized we had conflicting plans for the future. I wanted to live a traditional lifestyle, like what my parents have. Marriage, children, growing old together, then retiring and traveling the world. Joshua, however, was like a nomad. A free spirit. He wanted to pick up and catch a flight at the drop of a dime. Quit his job and live in different countries while living off of his savings. Stability wasn't his thing. Chasing after new experiences was. I tried to hang in there with him. But everything changed when I discovered he didn't want kids. That was the deal-breaker."

"Are children a must for you?"

"Yes, they absolutely are," Dani replied adamantly. "What about you?"

"Most definitely."

"Good."

A slow smile pulled at his lips, as if she'd just said she wanted to have children with him. He knew it was ridiculous to think of them starting a family together. But talk of having children somehow deepened the connection between them, as if he could feel the possibility buzzing between them.

"Now how about we put you back in the hot seat," Dani said. "Have you ever been in love?"

Von drew a long inhale, contemplating his answer carefully. "I have. But not as deeply as I'd like. You know that feeling they say you get when you know it's real? And you know you're with *the one*?"

"What, the butterflies, floating on air, head-in-the-clouds type of stuff?"

"Yes. All of that. That's what I want. And I'm willing to keep chasing it until I find it."

"Yeah, me, too," Dani rasped, her voice barely a whisper.

Maybe we've found it in each other, Von wanted to declare. His longing for her burned through him like a wildfire, each flame stoking his burgeoning feelings. Von fought the overwhelming urge to act on them as his efforts to remain cool slowly unraveled.

When Dani stretched her legs across the couch, he pressed his hands together, battling his desire to pull her closer. Her dress rose over her thighs. Rather than adjust it, she tilted her head back and drained her glass, leaving him teetering on the edge of restraint.

A drop of wine lingered on Dani's lip. Von's finger lightly traced the curve of her mouth before he gently wiped it away. "You spilled a little."

"Thank you…"

She leaned toward him, her supple breasts pressing against his chest. Unable to hold back any longer, Von covered her mouth with his. His tongue parted her lips, then slipped inside. Just as he worried she'd pull away, Dani slid onto his lap.

The kiss deepened as their tongues intertwined, twirling softly, then retreating, then melding once more. Von felt himself hardening between her legs. The soft warmth enveloped him, as if they were already connected in the most intimate way. His lips swept across her jawline and down to her neck, his teeth gently nibbling her skin. An insatiable moan vibrated deep within Dani's throat. When she drew him closer he freed her breasts, teasing her taut nipples with his mouth.

Dani's body trembled as her hips moved to the rhythm of his touch. Lifting her off the couch, he carried her into the bedroom. In between kisses, they pulled each other out of their clothes. Von attempted to pause for a beat. Stand back. Take in every inch of her stunning silhouette. But Dani wasn't having it. She reclined across the bed and pulled him in while kissing him with a fiery urgency. Her touch spoke louder than words ever could, conveying everything she hadn't said—their desire for each other was equally aligned.

But what Von felt for her was more than just a physical connection. Dani's presence evoked deep, emotional memories from their past. Back when he longed to break every rule written by their fathers and step over to the other side. Indulge in the thrill of her presence, despite it being taboo. And create a bond that he knew they were destined to share.

She was everything he'd ever wanted in a woman. Von just hoped she could get past their families' rivalry and give him a real chance. Because Dani had left him wondering whether or not he could be more than just her dirty little secret.

Chapter Eleven

Chloe reached across Dani's desk and handed her a mocha latte. "You never did answer my question."

"What question?" Her shrill tone a dead giveaway. Dani knew exactly what Chloe had asked. She just didn't want to respond.

"Please stop playing dumb with me. For the third time, why didn't you call me when you got home from the Zonian?"

"Good morning, Chief Miller!" Natalia called out on the way past her office. "How was your weekend?"

"It was pretty good. And yours?"

"Same!"

"Pretty good..." Chloe muttered under her breath. "Girl, between you leaving the bar with Von, the fact that you've been uncharacteristically vague during our text exchanges, and your skin looking all dewy this morning, there is something you're not telling me. And I wanna know what it is!"

"Listen, now that you're dating my brother, I've had to cut off some of your friendship privileges. Starting with me letting you in on every aspect of my personal life."

"But why? I haven't done anything to ruin your trust. Plus you know I don't tell Troy everything."

"Now how would I know that? You two have probably made some sort of pact, promising to keep your little pillow talks to yourselves."

"*Wrong.* I do still have a life outside of my relationship, Dani. Keep in mind that you and I were friends *long* before Troy and I started dating. Not to mention I don't believe in pillow talk. I'm an adult. I don't have to share every single thing with my partner."

"Okay, fine," Dani relented. "Close the door and I'll tell you everything."

Chloe sprang from her chair, pulled the door shut, then perched up on the edge of the desk. "All right, I'm listening. Spill it!"

"So, after Von and I left the Zonian, he insisted on walking me to my car. That turned into him following me home, which led to him coming inside."

"Wait, did he ask to come inside, or did you invite him in?"

"Von is a gentleman. He never would've asked. I invited him."

"Ooh!" Chloe exclaimed, leaning back so dramatically she almost tumbled off the desk. "Did I just hear you refer to Von Reed as a *gentleman*?"

"You know what? If this type of commentary is gonna go on throughout our conversation, then I'm going to end it right now—"

"No, no! Please, I'll stop. I promise. I'm just in shock right now. All my life, Von has been public enemy number one. So to go from that to hearing you invited the man inside your house is unreal."

"Well, if you think that's unreal, wait until I spill the tea on how the night ended. And how the morning began..."

"*Excuse* me?" Chloe screeched so loudly that within seconds, Troy came charging into the office.

"What's going on?" he huffed. "You two okay?"

"We're fine," Dani blurted before Chloe could say a word. "Your girlfriend was just being overly dramatic, per usual."

Troy's expression shifted from concerned to skeptical. "Are you sure that's all it is? Because the fact that neither of you can look me in my eye tells me that you're hiding something."

"Now that doesn't even sound like something we'd do," Chloe fired back. "And since when do I keep things from you, babe?"

"Is that even a real question? I know all about the whole girl code thing."

Dani gave him a dismissive wave. "I do appreciate you for checking on us. Now would you mind closing the door on your way out?"

"Should I take that as a not-so-subtle hint to leave?"

"Yes. You absolutely should."

"I've been kicked out of better places, you know," Troy joked, giving Chloe's shoulder an affectionate squeeze. "Are we still on for lunch at noon?"

"We are. But I need to make it quick. I've gotta get back home and edit my latest podcast episode."

"Ooh," Dani breathed, rubbing her hands together. "What's this one about?"

"It's a strange one. This case took place in the Midwest. It's about a group of friends who got together for game night, and the rules involved doing heavy drugs. After a few rounds of play, a few of them went outside to smoke cigarettes and never came back in. They were found the next day inside the homeowner's backyard, frozen to death."

"Damn," Troy said. "That is brutal. Where did this happen?"

"Right outside of Chicago. And yeah, it was brutal as hell considering it happened during the middle of winter. I'll let you both know when the episode is up so you can tune in. But anyway, I'll meet you at Autumn's Den at twelve—" Chloe stopped abruptly and slammed her palm against the desk.

"Wait, we're being rude. Dani, do you wanna come to lunch with us?"

"Oh…no. I—I can't. I already have plans."

"Since when do you have lunch plans?" Troy asked. "You usually just grab something from the vending machine and eat at your desk, or—"

"Babe," Chloe interrupted, tossing Dani a sly side-eye. "You know your sister is busy. Leave her alone. We'll schedule something for another time."

He backed out of the office, his head bobbing in an exaggerated nod. "Yeah, you two are definitely up to no good. But don't worry. I'm an excellent sleuth. I'll figure out what it is."

"*Or*," Dani said, "you could put those investigative skills to better use and help solve this case."

"And on that ornery note," he called out from the hallway, "Chloe, I'll see you at noon!"

The second his footsteps faded, Chloe jumped up and closed the door. "Anyway, so you and Von spent the night together, *and* you've got plans with him this afternoon?"

"Yes and yes."

"*Wooow…*this is unbelievable. I cannot believe you're sleeping with the enemy. Literally!"

"Well, after everything we did, he's not so much the enemy anymore. But hey, listen. You've gotta keep this under wraps. I don't want anybody to know about us. The investigation is all I want my squad to be focused on. If news gets out that Von and I are involved, that'll take the attention away from the case and bring a lot of scrutiny my way. And that's the last thing I need."

"Of course. You know your secret's safe with me. But here's my question. Is it safe with Von?"

Falling against the back of her chair, Dani retorted, "I would certainly hope so. I doubt that he'd want that attention on RPS.

Plus he should wanna stay under the radar since he believes these recent murders are targeted at him."

"*Should* being the operative word. But did you two actually establish that?"

"Not really, no. At one point, Von did joke about being my dirty little secret. However, we didn't get too deep into it."

"Well you've got to make that clear. I'd hate for miscommunication to stir up unnecessary drama and end things before they've even begun. Because honestly? You and Von have the potential to be great. He might even *the one...*"

Dani lowered her head and blew an exasperated groan. "Could you please slow down? Von and I literally just stopped hating each other. You're going from that to practically pushing us down the aisle?"

"See, now you're putting words in my mouth. I said no such thing. But from what I'm hearing, you two are moving at lightning speed. And I saw the way you were all cuddled up at the Zonian. Sharing drinks, slow dancing while whispering sweet nothings in each other's ears—"

Shooting up from her chair, Dani marched toward the door. "You should probably go home and change out of those yoga clothes so you won't be late for lunch with Troy. Why don't I walk you out?"

"I probably should. And I will. Right after you tell me what you and Von have planned this afternoon."

Dani's buzzing phone almost vibrated off the desk. Chloe caught it right before it toppled off the desk.

"Speaking of the devil," she said with a smirk while handing it over.

"I'm sure Von's just checking to make sure we're still on for today. He and I are actually going back to the Blanche Hotel to take another look at the crime scene. Then we're having lunch at the Sandstone Skybar afterward."

"Nice. Isn't that the hotel's rooftop café?"

"It is," Dani confirmed.

"Interesting choice. My former detective skills are telling me that you're the one who chose that place. And it's not because you love it. It's because you don't wanna be seen with Von. And since no one really goes there during the week except for out-of-towners, it's perfect. But if anyone *does* happen to see you there, they'll assume you two are discussing the case. Am I right?"

"Possibly."

"All right then. Do me a favor. Make sure you talk to Von about keeping whatever's going on between you two private. *Today.* Before wires get crossed, or expectations are misread, or word gets out and your relationship status ends up on the front page of *The Maxwell Times*."

Dani opened the door and stepped out into the hallway. "I will do that, friend. And even though you're being somewhat over-the-top right now, I appreciate the advice."

"Good. You're welcome. And hey, in all seriousness, it's been a long time since you've had someone good in your life. I know how much you've been wanting that. So I really am rooting for you two. Plus, you never know. Maybe this blossoming relationship will help mend your father's rift with Mr. Reed."

"We'll see. One thing at a time, though. Von and I have to actually *get* into a relationship first."

"Sounds to me like you're well on your way," Chloe said, leaning in for an embrace. "I'm happy for you. Now get back to work. I need to stop by Troy's desk before I leave, so don't worry about walking me out. I'll call you later."

Dani closed the door and practically floated to her desk. The flutters milling about inside her stomach hadn't stopped since her alarm went off that morning. Neither had thoughts of Von lying next to her, already awake as she'd gradually opened her eyes. The way he'd made slow, passionate love to her once more, their bodies moving in perfect harmony. Afterward he'd made coffee and omelets wearing nothing but a towel. It had been a long while since she'd had a man in her house, staying over and making meals. She'd forgotten how good it felt. It was all so surreal.

Looking forward to seeing you… she typed in response to his message.

Less than a minute passed before the phone vibrated against her palm. Excitement pulsated through her fingers as she gripped it tighter, anticipating his reply. But when she glanced at their text thread, there was no response from him. The last message in their chain was the one she'd just sent.

A small blue dot in the left corner indicated she had a new message. It had been sent from an unknown number.

Nice job catching Maxwell's first serial killer, Chief Miller. Now let's see if you can catch the second…

Chapter Twelve

Von stood in the middle of the Blanche Hotel's ladies' room, staring down at Dani's phone. The chilling text she'd received left him seething, triggering dark thoughts of violence. He was overcome with the need to protect her. To keep her out of harm's way—especially now that she'd finally let him in.

"Have you told your digital forensics investigator about this message yet?" Von asked.

"I haven't, but I will. I guess I'm hesitant because I already know what the answer's gonna be. And I don't want to hear him say that the message was sent from an untraceable burner phone."

"But I have heard that Chuck is special kind of tech wiz who can figure out pretty much anything. So just see what he says. You never know. You may get lucky."

"We'll see," Dani replied, her tone uneven as she slipped on a fresh pair of latex gloves. "But I'm not very hopeful. Which, ironically, is the same way I'm feeling about this crime scene. And that's probably my fault."

"Why is that?"

"I shouldn't have come here with such high expectations. My team and I did an extensive analysis of this place the night Brandy died. We didn't collect any viable evidence then. So I don't know why I'd come back today thinking things would be any different."

"Maybe you thought having a second pair of eyes would help—eyes that aren't a part of the Maxwell PD. Since I was trained outside of the police academy, I bring a completely different perspective. Plus my dad taught me a lot of what I know about forensics. So don't give up yet. We're not done here."

"Thanks for that," Dani replied, her faint tone sprinkled with distress. "I'll try. But it isn't easy. I can't believe I'm going through this again, so soon after last year's tragedy."

Silence took hold of the room as water dripped eerily from a porcelain sink. Von thought back on that night. The mayor's most pivotal event to date quickly morphed into a horror show. All that blood spattered across the textured pastel wallpaper. Law enforcement officers meticulously swabbing the surface, so hopeful they'd uncover vital DNA evidence. Paramedics scrambling to save Brandy's life, suctioning fluid from her airway while administering endless amounts of oxygen. Bloodied white cloths, strewn across the patterned stone floor as they'd struggled to stop the bleeding. The chilling possibility that their suspect was still on the scene, putting more lives at risk.

The woman who had discovered Brandy's lifeless body spent several days in the hospital, recovering from the trauma. The people of Maxwell were on edge, ready to abandon their hometown after it had once again come under attack. The police department faced relentless scrutiny as the pressure to name a suspect increased with each passing day.

Von could feel the tension closing in. The unsolved murders loomed over him heavily, as if he were a part of the force. But the growing threats against Dani kicked his need to help solve the case into high gear. Von still couldn't shake the feeling that the crimes were somehow directed at him. But there was no denying that the killer's motive was deeply rooted in a vendetta against her.

"We just need to find something," Dani said, shining her flashlight along the veiny marble tiles. "Even the tiniest bit of trace evidence that my team might have overlooked could lead us to the assailant."

Riffling through his forensics kit, Von pulled out an ultraviolet light. "It could. I'll use this to search the area again. Who knows. Maybe it'll pick up on bodily fluids that weren't in plain view or were hidden by other materials during the initial search."

"Good call. You may even find dried fluid that formed new patterns after being obscured by moisture."

"Let's hope…" Von switched off the restroom light and hit the power button on his device. A dark purple glow illuminated the space. He directed the beam toward the walls, the ceiling and the floor. "I know the restroom's been cleaned, but this light will detect fluid traces."

"Good. And just so you know, the blood that was collected from the crime scene belonged to the victim and no one else."

"What about the other evidence that was collected? Any fibers? Hair strands? Shoe impressions? *Anything* you could go on?"

"Nope," Dani confirmed. "Nothing that we were able to connect back to Brandy's murder."

"Humph," Von grunted, tossing the light back inside his kit, then grabbing a can of luminol spray. "You know, I hate to say this, but…"

"But what?"

"You may have to wait for another murder to occur."

"*Wow.* That is the exact same thing Chloe said. During her time with the Chicago PD, they occasionally had to use that tactic to track down their suspects."

"Yep. It's an unfortunate truth. Of course the best-case scenario would be you catch this maniac before another murder occurs. But consider the odds. No viable evidence was found at Lieutenant Edwards's crime scene. If we don't uncover anything here and no witnesses come forward, we'll be relying on the killer to slip up next time and leave behind a clue."

Dani look the bottle of luminol from his hand and sprayed it along the wall. "I'd hate for it to come down to that, but you both may be right."

The pair stood back, eyeing the wall while waiting to see if a blue glow would appear. A few faint areas glimmered under the chemical's pale crystalline, but nothing signaling bloodstains.

Tearing off her gloves, Dani raked her fingers through her hair. "This is so damn frustrating."

"Hey, come here..." Von placed his hands on her shoulders, gently massaging the tension from her muscles. "Don't get discouraged. You've done this before. You can do it again. And this time around, you've got a new heavy hitter on your team. We've just gotta keep digging. Our suspect can't keep this up for too long. Trust me, he's gonna slip eventually. And we'll be right there to take him down."

Her grumbling exhale indicated that she'd heard him, but wasn't completely convinced.

"What about Brandy's autopsy results?" he continued in a bid to pull her out of the funk. "Did the medical examiner discover anything significant?"

"Nothing that would lead us to a suspect. There was bruising along her upper back, arms and wrists, which would indicate a struggle. You already know about the stab wounds to the chest. There were eight to be exact. I was expecting for there to be some sort of cranial fractures to show she'd been struck in the head, which could explain how Brandy may have been subdued before the stabbing. But there were none."

"So the assailant must've sneaked up from behind and surprised her, leaving the victim no time to really put up a real fight."

"That's what I'm thinking," Dani said. "Brandy's hands were perfectly intact. No swelling or bruising. No traces of foreign skin cells underneath her fingernails. There were no signs of sexual assault, either, so this crime was not sexually motivated. Someone simply wanted Brandy Orland dead."

"Yes. But why? What enemies did she have? I dug pretty deep into her background. None of her reporting seemed salacious or worthy of her murder."

"Exactly," Dani said, her eyebrows shooting toward the ceiling as she tossed her gloves into a paper bag. "Which is why I don't believe the attack was about her."

"Point taken. Has the toxicology report come back yet? Maybe that'll tell us something. What that *something* is I don't know, but..." Von hesitated, staring up at the wall once again before turning the light back on. "I'm just grasping at straws here."

"At this point, we'll take any pieces of information we can get and hope that they fit the puzzle. I don't expect for toxicology to come back until sometime next week. Till then, like you said, we'll just have to keep digging."

"I'll continue to talk to my guys at RPS who were here on the scene and see whether there's anything they may have heard or observed that could be relevant. If I find anything out, I'll let you know."

"Thanks, Von. I'd appreciate that."

He braced himself, waiting for her to add a snide comment about his men hoarding information in an effort to be the hero. But she didn't, giving him hope that they'd turned a corner for good.

"I guess we can wrap things up here," Dani said.

Von's movements were heavy with disillusionment as he

packed up his kit. Failing to uncover promising new evidence wore on his confidence. But the weight of disappointment in Dani's muted tone triggered his savior complex. His fiery determination burned hotter than their frustration, fueling his resolve to keep going. He had to. For the sake of Dani and their hometown.

"Hey," Von said softly, "keep your head up. We're gonna stay in this until the work is done and the case is solved. You've got my word on that. Now, I hope you're still up for lunch. I already called ahead and asked Sandstone's bartender to whip up a pitcher of virgin mojitos for us since we're still on the clock. Once we're off work, I'll take you out for the real thing. How does that sound?"

"That sounds amazing," Dani murmured, punctuating the response with a soft kiss.

The touch of her lips was all Von needed to soothe the sting of defeat as they walked out the door.

Chapter Thirteen

There was no denying it. Dani was in over her head.

She blew an unsteady breath, watching as a stream of vapor billowed through the frigid air. Dani was planted on the high point of Cole's Ski Resort's Vesper Peak, also known as its max mountain. It was early Tuesday morning—almost two weeks since Brandy's murder. The ski area was fairly empty, as most guests were enjoying the resort's free continental breakfast buffet. But food was the last thing on Dani's mind. The thought of chocolate croissants and melon medleys churned her stomach. Her body needed movement—something invigorating that would leave her too exhausted to continue obsessing over the case.

Beams of sunlight shone across the tranquil pale blue sky, sparkling against a fresh blanket of snow. Majestic aspen and mixed fir trees lined the piste. Delicate whistles of western bluebirds drifted through the stillness. While she attempted to take in the beauty of it all, Dani's thoughts were overshadowed by her somber reality.

The state of the investigation was what lured her to the resort that morning. Cole's had always been her escape. A place of peace. And solitude. Somewhere she could go to get away from all the madness and think. Regroup. And refocus. There was a warm familiarity that had welcomed her since childhood, providing just the right amount of security. That was until Lieutenant Edward's dead body was found sprawled inside the stairwell.

The moment Dani had entered the main lodge, she shielded her eyes from the vestibule door, unable to bear the sight of it. Memories from that day sliced through her mind like a scalpel, each flashback cutting more meticulously than the last. The jagged, star-shaped bullet wound to the lieutenant's head. The fragments of gunpowder residue tattooed across his temple. The trauma of realizing some lunatic had intentionally killed a man she'd deeply admired. A man who'd been crucial to her professional journey and was a beloved pillar of the community.

Since that first murder, the gut feeling Dani got whenever trouble was brewing had been bubbling like lava, waiting to erupt. She was convinced that Lieutenant Edwards's murder, along with the ominous threats against her, were setting the stage for darker acts. Brandy Orland's tragic demise confirmed her worst fears.

Do not start obsessing...

The whole point of coming out to the resort was to unplug. But it was too late to press pause on her thoughts. They were already on a roll, running through her mind like a haunting montage. The chilling images of the night Brandy was murdered. Her body, sprawled underneath a row of sinks, immersed in a pool of blood…

"Stop it!" Dani screamed from the mountaintop, blowing exasperated puffs of air as the icy wind chilled her teeth. She bent forward, channeling her attention toward the blinding white snow. Forcing herself to shift the focus. Envision something positive. Something that was keeping her afloat amid the flood of madness.

Von...

Dani was still reeling from the unexpected turn her and

Von's relationship had taken. The whirlwind shift from sworn enemies to partners *and* lovers in such a short time had been both jarring and invigorating. His companionship was the balm that helped ease her stress. And his input had become an essential part of the investigation.

Unfortunately, those sentiments weren't shared by everyone. Animosity between Von's company and the Maxwell PD still lingered among some of their team members. Since the rivalry hadn't commenced overnight, Dani didn't expect it to come to an abrupt halt after one evening of pleasantries at the Zonian. Their joint social was a nice start. But creating peace would take time. And a resolution would require effort from both sides. For some, that was a lot to ask. Especially of their more resentful officers.

One thing Dani was grateful for was Von's open mind. He wasn't naive. He knew it was a possibility that one or more of his guys could be their suspect. When she mentioned it during their lunch at the Blanche Hotel, he didn't jump to their defense. Neither did she when Von brought up a member of the Maxwell PD being their suspect. She'd actually admitted to having the same thought.

"I'll tell you what," he told her. "If this keeps up, I will start secretly surveilling my employees. See if I can figure out whether or not it is in fact one of my guys. I'd suggest you do the same with your crew. Deal?"

"Deal," Dani had agreed.

Howling winds snapped her back to the moment as they swirled through the mountains' jagged peaks. She tightened the drawstrings on her bright red ski jacket, the breeze blowing all thoughts of the case from her mind. That was the magic of Vesper Peak. The steep, breathtaking slope may have been intimidating for some. But for her, it was pure solace.

Dani dug her steel poles into the powdery trail and pushed

off. Her heart raced to the rhythm of the skis cutting through the snow. Her strokes were swift and steady. The crisp pine air was intoxicating, injecting the thrill of the run with a euphoric high. She tightened her core. Leaned into the sharp turns, swaying from side to side as her knees absorbed the shock of each curve. The swoosh of her skis was melodic, easing her mind at every crest. Here, Dani was in control. Removed from her world and connected to nature. Able to think clearly. Contemplate who was after her. And why.

The rush down the piste grew faster. The speed was invigorating. Affirming. Alerting her that answers would soon come. With Von's help, she was getting closer to the truth.

Gravity took hold as snowflakes shimmered along the trail. For the first time in a long time, she felt a semblance of tranquility. A flash of freedom before the storm of the case descended upon her once she hit the base. Her breathing quickened. She inhaled the exhilaration and exhaled adrenaline, puffs of air fogging her goggles.

Her bliss was momentarily disrupted by a black dot appearing briefly through the corners of her eyes. Another lone skier, emerging from a cluster of lodgepole pines.

Whoosh!

Every muscle in Dani's body tensed as her right ski slipped across a mogul hidden within the snow. Shifting her weight forward, she turned the edge of her ski against it, rebalancing herself.

Stay centered, her inner voice whispered. No matter how many times she'd skied it, Vesper Peak was still a challenge.

Gripping her poles tighter, Dani eyed the winding trail up ahead. She leaned into the steep terrain, tucking the sticks under her arms as that pulse-pounding rush returned.

A shadow flickered, pulling her attention away once more.

It hovered to her right. A swift glance revealed the skier she'd seen moments ago. He was catching up.

Dani's intuition kicked in, its intensity as suffocating as the thin mountain air. Sensing an imminent threat, she contemplated slowing her descent. Allowing the skier to pass her by. Because something wasn't right.

Maybe you're just being paranoid...

Dani reminded herself that she didn't own the slope. Another skier had the right to be on it. Yet that rationale failed to decrease the anxiety clenching her chest. She searched the mountain for other skiers. There were none. She and this dark figure were alone. The empty, wide-open clearing only amplified his ominous presence.

Her need to get off the slope grew urgent. Dani's feet widened as she bent down, tucking her body into a low stance while pressing her elbows against her sides. As her speed increased, so did the other skier's. The swish of their skis grew louder. Dani could no longer see him. Because he was directly behind her.

Her legs deadened as the impact of each bump rattled her joints. Determined to stay on her feet, Dani forced herself to keep cool calm. This could be nothing.

It could also be something. Something treacherous...

The base of the mountain appeared up ahead. A rush of relief shot up her calves as the numbness began to wear off. Dani's grip on the poles loosened just enough for her fingers to regain feeling.

You're almost there...

The picturesque wintery landscape blurred. Dani poured every ounce of her energy into reaching the bottom of the mountain.

Get there...get there!

Her determination faltered when a massive snow cloud engulfed her. The funnel of powdery dust sent her senses spiraling. Once the drift settled, that dark, hovering figure appeared next to her, expertly maneuvering the piste.

Startled, Dani pulled her skis inward, attempting to change directions. She almost lost her footing mid-switch.

Reset!

Her legs began to fold like tattered branches, succumbing to the weight of distress. Digging her poles into the snow, Dani regained her balance while picking up speed. So did the other skier, who moved with the same expertise.

As the pair raced down the mountain, Dani eyed a quick flash of silver. She attempted to scream. But the pounding in her throat silenced her.

The skier swung an arm through the air. A sharp, stinging pain hit Dani's torso. The impact sent her flailing, her skis cutting erratically through the snow as she struggled to stay on her feet.

"I've been hit," she panted, even though no one was around to hear her. "I've been hit!"

The cold, searing pain was unbearable. Bobbing back and forth on her skis, Dani fought the urge to fall to her knees. Unwavering determination took over, pushing her through the agony.

Just when her attacker swung an arm in the air, Dani stabbed him in the groin with her pole. He doubled over, emitting an animalistic growl in the process. She seized the moment and took off.

A treacherous curve came into view. Angling her skis sharply, Dani cut a high-speed turn that sent her skidding along its edge, leaving a plume of snow in her wake. She attempted to recover. But not before the hiss of her attacker's approach echoed from behind.

The pain in Dani's side took hold. Fighting the impulse to

give in, she gritted her teeth, resolute in making it out alive. Her descent became a blur of agony. Ignoring the crackle of her assailant's skis nipping at her heels, she pressed on with renewed urgency.

You're almost there. Just keep going...

With a final burst of energy, Dani made it to the bottom of the mountain, practically plowing into the patrol office door.

"Help me, please!" she screamed. "Somebody help me!"

The second an officer came rushing out, her assailant made an abrupt U-turn.

"Ma'am," he said, "are you all right? Did you injure yourself on the slope?"

"No," Dani moaned, barely able to breath. "I was… I was attacked. By him." She pointed in the direction of the suspect. Her glove hand wavered at the sight of him disappearing into a cluster of mixed firs. "You've gotta go—go after the person who…"

Dani paused, her head spinning faster than the flurries whipping around her. Disoriented, she struggled to focus on her surroundings. "Wait. I was…he was just…"

"I'm sorry, ma'am," the patrol officer said. "Go after the person who did what?"

"I—can you…call Von Reed," Dani muttered before falling to her knees and collapsing into the snow.

Chapter Fourteen

Von charged down the hallway toward Dani's hospital room, checking the number near the door before knocking.

Pull it together. Straighten your face. Don't lose your composure...

"Come in!" she called out.

He turned the handle slowly, sticking his head inside before entering.

"Hey, how are you?" he asked quietly, hoping his soothing tone would mask the alarm coursing through his body.

"I'm all right," Dani said, barely turning toward him as she lay propped up against a stack of pillows. "A bit banged up, but I'll be fine. The doctor said the worst of it is the superficial stab wound that barely penetrated my abdomen. I've got my ski coat's synthetic polyester fill to thank for that."

"I'm so sorry, Dani. But it sounds like you got really lucky. So for that, I'm glad. I had no idea you were even going skiing at Cole's today. Had I known, I would've gone with you."

"It was a last-minute thing. I just needed to do something that would take my mind off the investigation. You know, get some alone time in to clear my head. Figure out the next steps..." Her voice drifted as she swiveled robotically, wincing with each movement of her body. "Why are you just standing there in the doorway? Come in. Have a seat. Listen to me complain about this nightmare of a day."

Von shuffled farther into the room, squinting as slivers of sunlight peeked through the half-drawn blinds. He hauled a heavy wood-framed chair toward the bed and took a seat, his eyes on the television rather than Dani. Focusing on an old episode of *Living Single* would be easier than admitting that he wasn't fond of hospitals.

The stark white walls, blur of lab coats, pungent odor of antiseptic and shrill beeping monitors brought back unpleasant childhood memories. Von had spent countless hours at Cedar Ridge Hospital with his mother during her nephrology appointments and dialysis treatments. After she'd received a kidney transplant, the incessant visits continued once complications arose. It had taken doctors months to figure out the correct course of immunosuppressant drugs. Once they did, she was finally able to live a normal life, and the hospital visits became less frequent.

"We've gotta catch this bastard, Von."

"Yes… I know we do." Finally turning to her, he studied Dani's expression. Her face appeared drawn, tight with worry, each crease deepening as she spoke. Unshed tears pooled in her dim eyes. Her lips quivered, as if holding back words she was hesitant to speak.

"Ow," she wheezed, dabbing a quarter-size bruise splayed across her right temple.

Von jolted to his feet so quickly that the chair almost toppled over. "Are you okay? Should I call the nurse? Do you need more pain meds, or numbing cream for that?"

"No, I'm fine. What I need is to get the hell out of here. Get back on the street so I can hunt down this psychopath who tried to kill me."

"Shouldn't they be keeping you overnight? At least for observation?"

"I certainly hope not. Even if they try, I'm not staying."

The defiance in her toned prompted Von to pull the chair in closer and sit back down. “Listen, Dani. I’ve been thinking about everything. These attacks on you. The murders. The security of Maxwell, the community’s diminishing faith in the police department… I think it’s time that we switch gears. Step up our game. Create a new plan that could actually take down the suspect. One that won’t require us to have to wait until another murder occurs.”

“I’ve been thinking about all that, too. And I totally agree. In the meantime, I’ve got Troy and a few other officers reviewing the surveillance footage from the slopes today. They’re at Cole’s now, looking for witnesses who may have seen something. And we’ll be sending my ski gear to the crime lab so they can process it for DNA evidence.”

“Good. I hope something comes of it. Remember how we talked about surveilling our teams more closely to find out whether one of our own is behind all this?”

“I do.”

“Well, I think it’s time for us to put that plan into action. We need to put a couple of our employees who we can trust to work. Get them to spark up some *just between us* types of conversations around the office. Surveilling their movements is one thing, but getting inside their heads could give us the answers we’re looking for, too. Alert us to who knows what and who’s up to what. If one of our team members is the culprit, I highly doubt that he hasn’t bragged about it or dropped some sort of hint to someone.”

Dani shot straight up, gripping her left shoulder in the process. “*Ouch.* I like that idea. You and I could also start keeping a closer eye on our officers around the office. See if any of them are behaving strangely toward us, or just acting differently than normal. That goes for in person and on social media. You know how people love to post cryptic memes about what they're going through. We may luck up and find a few clues that way. I'm also not above putting GPS trackers on the cars of any officers who appear suspicious."

Whipping out his phone, Von launched the Notes app. "Those are some great suggestions. I'll keep a record of them."

His fingers sprinted across the keys, racing to keep pace with the whirlwind of ideas being tossed out. After several minutes, the steady rhythm of Dani's monitor morphed into a series of frantic, high-pitch beeps. Von glanced up at the screen. Her heart rate had increased to 115 beats per minute.

"Hey, Dani," he whispered, hoping his gentle tone would calm her energy. "Why don't we table this conversation for later and just focus on your recovery? We've got plenty of time to talk about the investigation."

"Actually, no. We don't."

"Look, your health comes first. What happened to you today was traumatic, both physically and emotionally. Your officers are perfectly capable of managing the case while you recuperate. And of course they'll have RPS's full support, too."

Dani's lips parted and shut repeatedly, as if she wanted to debate but couldn't find the words. Eventually, her icy scowl thawed, melting into a soft expression of acceptance. Falling back against the pillows, she uttered, "I hear you, Von. And I appreciate your concern, it's just hard for me to sit back and relinquish control. You know me. I think I can handle everything at all times."

Tread carefully, he reminded himself before taking her hand in his. "I know you do. And you probably can. But right now, it's important for you to do what's best for *you*. And that means falling back a bit and taking care of yourself. You've got a ton of perfectly capable people around you who are more than willing to take charge temporarily. Plus… I care about you, Dani. More than you know. It shook me to my core when ski patrol called and told me you had been injured. As soon as I heard those words, I knew you'd been attacked. The thought of you being in that type of danger yet again really—"

As his voice broke, Dani's grip on his hand tightened.

"Trust me, Von, I understand. I'm shaken up, too. But I'm not backing down. I can't. That's what this maniac wants. I won't let him win. Especially not now. The stakes are too high."

"Dani, please, listen to me—"

Her raised hand was all it took to silence him. "I'm sorry, but you can't talk me out of this. Now, I get it. Until the killer is caught, I can't move around town like I normally do. So I won't. But you need to trust that I can work and recover at the same time. I can't let up. If anything, it's time to push even harder."

A heavy silence fell over them. Von glanced up at the monitor. Dani's heart rate had normalized, dropping down to ninety-six beats per minute.

"Please stop watching that monitor like I'm about to flatline," she insisted, running her fingertips along his forearm. "I promise you, I'm okay."

"I know you are. And I hear everything you're saying. You're a pro. So I get it. And I'll back off. But what I will *suggest*, however, is that you stick to your word and move around town differently. More cautiously. And never let your guard down. You're so used to being our police chief that you've forgotten you're still a target. The minute you let your defenses slip, you leave yourself wide open for anything to happen."

With a slight nod, Dani replied, "You're right. And I will take heed."

"See, that's what I wanna hear. Because together, we got this. I'll be right by your side through it all. And not just as your security-slash-investigative consultant, either. I, um… I'd like to be something more. If you'll let me…"

Dani's gaze drifted toward the window as her grip on his hand loosened.

"Uh-oh," Von muttered. "Did I say something wrong?"

"No, you didn't. We just need to talk about what you're asking of me."

The mood in the room shifted. Their spirited conversation became overshadowed by her somber reaction. Sliding his hand out from underneath hers, Von said, "Why do I get the sense that you really are trying to keep me a secret?"

"That sounds so harsh. It really isn't like that—"

"What is it like then?"

"I just don't think it would be a good idea for us to go public with our relationship. At least not right now. I need for Maxwell PD's sole focus to be on this case. Not my love life. If we start dating out in the open, I'm convinced we'd be a distraction that might throw off the entire investigation. And that goes for RPS, too."

"Dani, we're adults. Almost everyone on your team is either married or in a relationship. The same goes for mine. So why should we be denied that? We have a right to be happy, don't we? Plus, last I checked, we're the leaders of our organizations. Why would we allow our personal lives to be dictated by our subordinates? And if somebody *were* to step out of line over what we do in our private time, they'd be dealt with accordingly."

"You're right," she replied in a hushed tone while picking at the label on her hospital bracelet. "But I would also hate for our situation to shift the focus away from the victims. On top of that, I'm already in the killer's crosshairs. If we take our relationship public, that could end up putting you in danger, too."

"Or maybe you and I coming together would be viewed as

a power move. We'd become formidable allies. Because think about it. If the killer is one of our own, they're probably loving the fact that we're enemies and our agencies have been at odds. That puts part of our focus on the rivalry rather than the case. If we're together, *that* changes the game."

"In terms of the case? Yes. But on a personal level, I'm sorry, but I disagree."

Rubbing his temples in frustration, Von asked, "What if we do everything in our power to keep this situation under wraps, and somebody finds out about us anyway?"

"I don't know. We can cross that bridge when we get to it. If we ever do."

His fallen expression shifted from frustration to resignation. "Is that what this is really about? Or does it have something to do with your family, and you not wanting to disappoint them by getting involved with me?"

Her silence was all the answer he needed.

"Wooow," Von breathed, grasping the arms of his chair before slowly standing.

"Wait, are you leaving?"

"No," he retorted while pacing the floor. "I just—I'm thinking…"

"Listen, I think we're focusing on the wrong thing. Let's get back to the real issue at hand. Apprehending the killer."

"Agreed." Stopping abruptly, Von turned and faced Dani. "Actually, why don't we put this situation between us on the back burner and revisit it once an arrest has been made?"

The second he made the suggestion, Von's chest caved, as if the words shot holes straight through his heart.

"You mean stop seeing each other romantically?"

"Yes."

"I don't know," Dani rasped, her tone tinged with sadness. "Is that really what you want?"

"Of course not. But when it comes to this case, if you think that would be best, then yes."

Dani's cell phone lit up, its hard-shell case vibrating loudly against the wooden tray table.

"That's Troy," she said after swiping it open. "He and Chloe just checked in at the registration desk. They're on their way up."

"Okay, well, I'll leave then…give you all a chance to talk privately."

"Von, you know you don't have to go."

"No, it's fine. I'll check on you later. Let me know if they decide to release you today and I'll come back and pick you up. Unless you'd rather have Troy take you home."

Slowly extending an arm, Dani gestured for Von to come closer. He obliged, taking her hand in his.

"I'd love for you to come back and get me. I'll call you when Troy and Chloe leave. Thank you for coming. I really appreciate you. And I hope our conversation didn't upset you."

"I'm good," he lied, brushing a kiss across her forehead. "We'll talk later."

"Hey," Dani said, gently pulling him back when he began walking away. "You do understand where I'm coming from with all this, don't you?"

"I do. But it still doesn't make it any easier. Anyway, I'm gonna go. I know you don't want your brother to see me here. I'll call you."

"Von, please. I just…"

He hesitated, waiting to hear her response. But when her voice faded, Von realized that Dani had no real argument left. Familiar voices out in the hallway sent him ducking out of the room and toward the stairwell, avoiding the elevator to steer clear of Troy and Chloe.

Confliction weighed heavily on his conscience as he bolted

down the stairs and trudged through the expansive sunlit lobby. The bright surroundings were a stark contrast to his own inner turmoil. A vision of him and Dani lying in bed together just days ago felt like a distant memory. In its place was the professional bond they'd built, alongside the promise to keep fighting for what mattered most—bringing the killer to justice. If that meant suspending their intimate relationship for the sake of the case, then so be it.

Nevertheless, the sharp sting of that decision lingered, a painful reminder of the boundaries they couldn't cross.

Chapter Fifteen

Dani readjusted the bustline on her red silk cocktail dress and glanced around Gibson Country Club's elegant dining hall. The château-style room had been transformed into an elaborate art gallery in celebration of the club's annual auction.

Vibrant oil paintings on canvas, handblown glass sculptures and framed black-and-white photographs surrounded tables that were meticulously set with fine china and crystal stemware. A live string quartet positioned near the entrance performed soft classical music. Waitstaff glided through the crowd, offering champagne flutes that sparkled like stars underneath elegant chandeliers. The who's who of Maxwell mingled with the club's affluent members, who'd come together to support local artists and charities. It was a spectacular occasion that Dani seldom missed, as her family had been close with the Gibsons for over two decades.

It'd been quite some time since Dani had donned a fancy gown and attended an upscale event. She had been so wrapped up in the case that her personal life had taken a back seat—with the exception of her dalliances with Von. They hadn't spent much time together since she'd been released from the hospital a little over a week ago. He still checked in with her through text messages and sporadic phone calls. But the conversations had primarily been about the investigation.

Hitting a rough patch so soon after they'd finally reconciled didn't sit well with Dani. Their intimate nights together only complicated matters. Yet despite missing Von, the facts remained the same. A relationship between them would draw too much attention. And after all the drama their connection had stirred between them, Dani realized now was not the time to get swept up in an affair. Their focus had to stay on the case. There would be plenty of time for them to pursue something more once they caught the killer.

If Von's still interested, a nagging voice rebutted.

Dani's red satin pumps clicked across the polished hardwood floor, her toes tensed in anticipation of a confrontation. She hadn't realized RPS was handling security for the event and ran into Von the moment she'd arrived. Dani attempted to ignore the cloud of awkwardness looming over them when they greeted each other. But after she'd extended a hand to him, Von's snarky chuckle was a clear indication of his mood.

His posture had been rigid, and there was a sadness behind his eyes that seemed to linger even as his gaze drifted from her lips down to her breasts. Von's formal greeting, "Good evening, Chief Miller," felt worlds apart from the warmth of their recent exchanges. The chilliness in his tone assured her that she wasn't imagining the tension between them. Troy and Chloe had picked up on it, too, their raised eyebrows proof of the palpable strain.

"*Hey*," Chloe had whispered the moment Von walked off, "why is he acting so strange toward you? I hope he's not trying to pull back. Especially not now, after you two have been… you know…"

Dani remained silent, not in the mood to rehash their conversation at the hospital. Plus she'd needed a minute to cool off. To come down off of the high of seeing Von. Tonight, there was no denying that the man looked more handsome than she cared to admit. His expertly tailored tuxedo accentuated his muscular physique to perfection. A fresh haircut framed his handsome face. The scent of spicy sandalwood pulsated from his neck, stirring something deep within her. It was the same cologne he'd worn the first night they'd made love.

"Dani!" Chloe called out, interrupting her thoughts as she approached the bar. "I've been looking all over for you. Are you okay?"

"I'm fine. Why?"

"Well, I'm assuming you're irritated after Von came at you with that dry *good evening* when you got here. And now he and Kevin are standing over there staring at us like we're under surveillance."

Dani's turned discreetly, peering at the men through the corners of her eyes. Sure enough, their gazes were fixed on them. Her mouth went dry at the thought of an actual fall-out between her and Von. It would be her worst nightmare—their relationship going sour due to the fact that they'd slept together.

"Von better not have spilled a word to Kevin about what happened between us."

"Considering he's his best friend, I'd bet the house that he did. And let's not forget, you told me. So to be fair, neither of you kept it a secret, *if* he's guilty of running his mouth."

"Chloe, please. Now is not the time to try to rationalize with me. Let's walk around and get out of their direct view before I get irritated."

Dani fought the urge to look back and see if Von was still watching her. She and Chloe strutted toward the center of the room, pausing at an elaborate buffet table filled with savory hors d'oeuvres, beautifully arranged sushi and mouthwatering pastries. Nearby, several bartenders worked at mixing stations, chatting with guests while crafting signature cocktails.

"I really want a cosmopolitan," Dani said. "But I'd better

stick to something nonalcoholic. Even though I'm off duty, I get the feeling that everybody is judging me. I hope nobody tries to question me about the case."

"Yeah, that would be rude. If they do, just hit them with a *no comment*. Anyway, speaking of the case, any updates from the crime lab?"

"Nothing useful. You already know we didn't get solid evidence back on the first two murders. And there wasn't any foreign DNA left on my clothing after the attack at Cole's. Surveillance cameras didn't capture anything that would identify the suspect since the attack occurred so far up Vesper Peak. And I swear, that psycho must be some sort of professional mountain climber. Because we're thinking he escaped off the side of the ski slope."

"Damn. Who the hell are we dealing with here? And what could his motive possibly be?"

"That's the million-dollar question. We just can't figure out the answer. Think about last year's killer. We never could have predicted his identity. It came as a complete shock. This one might be just as surprising. Or, maybe not…"

"What do you mean, maybe not?" Chloe asked, piling sashimi onto a plate.

Dani tossed a few mini spring rolls inside a napkin, then headed toward a high-top table. On the way there, she glanced over at the rustic limestone fireplace where Von and Kevin had been posted up. Kevin was gone. But Von was still standing there, watching her intently. When their eyes met, his expression softened. The warmth in his gaze curled her lips into a subtle smile.

"Oh, well," Chloe said. "And just like that, the two starstruck lovers have forgiven each other."

"You don't miss a thing, do you?"

"Dani, I am a highly trained former Chicago PD detective. Does that answer your question?"

"Yes, it does. But you've been nosy all your life, friend. So let's not act like your training with the force gave you that skill. Anyway, as I was saying. Motive. I'd *like* to think that no one has issues with me. However, that's clearly not true. We've talked about bitter officers on the force. And even though we had a great time at the joint social, all isn't well with RPS. Von keeps insisting that the murders are connected to him, but I'm not convinced. How would that explain the attacks on me?"

"Let me ask you this. Are you convinced that the murders are connected to the attacks?"

"Oh, most definitely," Dani affirmed. "Without a doubt."

Chloe bit down on a slice of salmon, then looked over her shoulder. "What about Kevin? Have you ever thought of him as a suspect?"

"No," Dani said slowly, her features tightening with confusion. "Kevin may not be my favorite person in the world, but he and I have never had any real issues. And if this is some sort of dual attack against both Von and me, I don't think Kevin would do anything to hurt him. They've been best friends for as long as I can remember."

"Yeah, well, things change. Relationships shift. Von runs RPS, which means he's in a position of power. He's Kevin's boss. I'm sure that's not always easy—balancing the friendship and work relationship. So you never know. Maybe something went down between them and Kevin is trying to sabotage the company to get back at Von."

"I mean, it could be, but…that's a pretty wild assumption to make considering there's nothing to back it up. And what does that have to do with me?"

"You don't think Von has talked about you to Kevin? He's been crushing on you since high school. He and Kev have probably dissected everything about you—from your family to Mr. Miller's position with the Maxwell PD. Bottom line? Kevin knows Von has feelings for you. So that's how this situation is connected to you. Now, I may be grabbing at straws here, but if Kevin's jealous of Von's success, jealous of the Maxwell PD's success, envious that his best friend is into the woman who's been the enemy…that's all the motive he'd need to be your suspect."

Dani slowly nodded while scanning the room. "Who knows, you could be right. Considering we don't have any suspects, I can't afford to court anybody out. So I won't dismiss your theory. By the way, where is Kevin?"

"I have no idea. Von is still standing alone over by the fireplace, staring you down. Maybe Kevin left."

A loud buzz swept over the room as the auctioneer stepped onto a small stage near the front of the room. The crowd whispered excitedly, gesturing at various art pieces while getting their paddles in position. When the stout, balding man held a hand in the air, a hush fell over the crowd.

"Hello, ladies and gentlemen!" he boomed into the mic. "Welcome to Gibson Country Club's twenty-second annual art auction, where your winning bids will benefit independent artists as well as several organizations, including Maxwell Children's Hospital and the Reed Center for Rehabilitation. My name is Curtis Feldman, and I'll be your bid caller for the evening. On behalf of the Gibson family, I would like to thank you all for being here, and express just how much your generosity means to them. With that being said, let the auction begin!"

The crowd erupted into a frenzy of applause. As the ovation faded, a blood-curdling scream tore through the room. In an instant, panic gripped the audience. People bolted in every direction, a sea of frantic bodies scrambling toward the exits.

Amid the chaos, Von charged Dani, his swift steps cutting through the mayhem. "Are you okay?"

"Yes, I'm fine. *We're* fine," she said, grabbing hold of Chloe. "But apparently somebody else isn't. We need to figure out what's going on."

"Help!" someone yelled. "We need assistance out on the golf course!"

"The golf course?" Dani repeated, her eyes darting with confusion. "Why would anybody be out there? It's pitch black, and the fairway is closed."

She and Chloe followed Von onto the terrace. Their shoes pounded the rich gray stone as they approached the wrought iron railing overlooking the green.

"What is going on out here?" Troy asked, rushing toward the group. "I was inside the cigar lounge and heard all this screaming."

"That's what we're trying to figure out," Dani told him. "We can't see a thing. It's too dark."

"On the way out here, I heard Mr. Gibson say he's gonna turn on the lights and figure out what's happening."

Suddenly, the range lit up. A wave of screams rippled across the terrace. There, near the eighteenth hole, lay a body sprawled underneath the flagstick.

Chapter Sixteen

Von followed closely behind Dani as she charged the stairs and ran across the fairway.

"Troy!" she yelled. "Call for backup!"

A frantic rush ensued when guests rushed onto the green. "Everyone," Von called out, holding his arms out at his sides, "I'm going to need for all of you to go back inside. This is official police business. We need to stay out of the way and let the Maxwell PD do their jobs."

RPS officers stepped in and began ushering the onlookers back toward the stairwell.

"This cannot be happening," Dani said, hovering over the man lying on the ground. "This *cannot* be happening..."

Von joined her, peering down at him. He appeared to be in his mid-thirties. His strong, sculpted features—smooth, unlined and seemingly familiar—were frozen in an unsettling look of shock. His dark gray tuxedo was still in immaculate condition, not a wrinkle or speck of dirt in sight. There didn't seem to be any signs of a struggle or trauma. No bruising or wounds were apparent. No blood was present. And no weapons were in the vicinity.

Dani sprang into action and performed chest compressions as sirens wailed in the distance.

"He's not breathing," she panted. "And he doesn't have a pulse."

Von's stomach pulled at the look of alarm on Dani's face. "Keep trying. The paramedics will be here any minute. I wonder if the guy had a heart attack or something along those lines, since I'm not seeing any signs of trauma."

"Yeah, maybe he wasn't feeling well and wanted to get some fresh air, or..."

As her voice trailed off, Troy took a knee and stared at the victim. "Wait, isn't this—"

He was interrupted when a group of police officers and paramedics rushed down the fairway.

"Hey, let's give these guys some room!" Dani yelled before stepping away. Crossing her arms over her chest, she turned to Troy. "Yes, that's him."

"Wait, you two know this man?" Von asked.

Before responding, she asked Troy, "Can you and the other officers cordon off the area? And grab a forensics kit from your car for me?"

"Of course. Be right back."

Von waited for Dani to answer his question. She didn't, her eyes still fixated on the victim as paramedics quickly moved in. One of them pulled out a portable monitor, the device blinking to life with a series of beeps. Another cut open the man's shirt and swiftly attached the electrodes to his bare chest. The screen flickered, then displayed a flat line.

When Dani released a ragged stream of air, Von gently grasped her shoulder as they continued to look on.

"Let's check for a pulse," the paramedic said after readjusting the leads. She pressed her fingers against the side of his neck. Several moments passed before a shadow of worry flickered across her face.

"Okay, clear!" another paramedic shouted. He hit the button on the defibrillator. "One, two, three!" he counted, pressing the paddles against the victim's chest. Electricity surged through the cables. The monitor's screen flashed again. Another flatline.

"Damn it," Dani huffed, turning away.

"Hey," Von said, wrapping his arm around her. "Come here. Are you all right?"

"No, I'm not."

"I understand. But hang in there. I know this isn't easy to watch, but from the looks of things, you may not have another murder victim on your hands—*if* the victim is actually dead. At least we're not seeing any outward signs of violence."

"That's true," Dani responded just as Troy approached with the forensics kit. "But I don't want to get my hopes up, so we'll see what happens."

"One thing's for sure, though. If this man is in fact dead, and foul play is involved? That would mean we've got yet another murder on our hands that occurred while RPS was on duty."

Dani remained silent.

"I know you haven't really bought into that theory," Von continued. "But you can't keep denying that these crimes are aimed at me. The suspect has killed someone at every major event RPS has recently worked."

"You know what else can't be denied?"

"What's that?"

"The fact that the victim is my ex-boyfriend."

Von's lungs emptied as he let off a stunned gasp. "I—I'm sorry. The victim is your *what*?"

"My ex-boyfriend. His name is Jeffrey Simmons. We dated for a few months, but the attraction just wasn't there. He and I remained good friends and still hung out on occasion. So, yeah. If he was killed, I'm dealing with yet another murder that's connected to me, too."

Her words triggered an intense urge deep within Von. His

body grew tense while fighting the need to pull Dani close. Hold her until the fear disappeared from her eyes. He longed to brush aside the stray curls framing her face and tell her everything would be okay. But he couldn't. Not here. Not now. Despite the lines between them already being crossed, she'd made it clear that no public displays of affection would be tolerated.

"I should get to work," she said, slipping on a pair of gloves, then pulling a flashlight from the kit.

"Hey, Chief!" Troy called out from the brush near the side of the course. "You need to see this."

Von followed Dani as she rushed toward him.

"What's up?" she huffed. "What'd you find?"

Troy raised his hand in the air, the moonlight glinting off a sharp needle.

"Is that…a *syringe*?"

"It is. And I think we should get it sent to the crime lab first thing in the morning. As a matter of fact, I'll drive it down myself."

"Good idea. I'd love to know if it's somehow connected to Jeffrey."

"If it is," Von interjected, "that could explain why there's no obvious signs of trauma."

"Exactly," Troy replied, taking a step back. "I'll pack it up now."

"Chief Miller?" one of the paramedics called out.

"Yes?" she replied, her voice strained as she and Von rushed back over. "How's he doing?"

"Not good. There's still no pulse. We should get him to the hospital as soon as possible."

"Yes, thank you," Dani whispered, her head dropping toward the ground.

Von discreetly pressed his hand against the small of Dani's back. Something told him she could use the support. He braced himself, waiting for her to nudge him away. Instead, he felt her body relax against his palm.

"Hey," she whispered. "Let's talk. In private."

He trailed behind her to a secluded spot nestled near the side of the fairway. Dani's lips parted, but instead of speaking, she pressed her fingertips against her temples and stared off into a cluster of cottonwood trees.

"You good?" he asked.

When she finally spoke up, her voice was barely audible over the fluttering leaves. But Von heard her loud and clear when she said, "Not only do I think we're dealing with another serial killer here, but I think he's a pro. Better yet, we might be dealing with a group of pros."

"A group? So you think these murders are being committed by more than one person?"

"Possibly. Or maybe I'm just reaching. But how can one person continue to get away with these crimes at such public locations? During these crowded events, without *anybody* seeing something? I mean, it's as if the killer has eyes everywhere, and the person knows exactly when to strike without being noticed."

"You could be right. Especially when you consider there hasn't been any evidence left at the scenes. That would be hard to pull off if this was just a solo operation."

"*And* if the suspect, or suspects, didn't have a background in law enforcement..." Dani paused, clutching the sides of her face. "Hopefully the syringe Troy found will be the first real break in this case. But who knows? That needle could've been used by one of the golfers to inject insulin or something. So we can't bank on that just yet. I need to make sure doctors look for signs of a puncture wound that may have been caused by a needle. I want a toxicology screening done, too.

I'm anxious to find out if Jeffrey was injected with some sort of drug or poison."

"I'll be sure to remind you of all that in case you forget."

Dani gave him a nod, then walked back over to him, her arms curled protectively against her chest. "I need to jump in and help the team. Would you mind going inside and taking the temperature of the crowd? I'm curious to know what's being said and whether anybody saw anything."

"Absolutely. I'll check back in with you soon."

Von backed away slowly, the soles of his black leather oxfords biting into the turf as he retreated. He had every intention on fulfilling the request. But he was having a hard time tearing himself away from Dani. He wanted to stay by her side. Comfort her. Look after her, even though she didn't think she needed any of that. Von was convinced she would later, when the dust settled and the scene at Gibson's was fully processed. Everyone would go their separate ways, and she'd have to return to her place alone.

Not on my watch...

Walking back over, Von tapped Dani's shoulder.

"Listen," he said, wincing at the grim intensity in her expression. "After we leave here, I don't want you to be by yourself—"

"Von, please. I'm not thinking about anything beyond this moment. I've got to stay focused and sort through this scene."

"I understand that, but when all this is—"

He was interrupted by the buzz of his cell phone. A text from Kevin flashed across the screen.

I stepped out of the club for a minute and just walked back into chaos. Somebody fainted out on the golf course? What's going on??

"Damn, word travels fast..." Von muttered, not realizing Dani was staring over his shoulder.

"So Kevin wasn't here when this happened to Jeffrey, *allegedly...*" she said.

The skepticism slicing through her tone didn't go unnoticed. "Apparently not."

"Humph. Interesting. Take this however you want, but I don't trust Kevin. We need to keep an eye on him."

"Wait, you're suspicious of *Kevin*?" Von shot back. "As in my vice president of RPS, Kevin Freelain?"

"Yes, him. Let's talk more about it later. But just know that I have my suspicions."

Von stood there, too stunned to move, let alone respond.

Another text from Kevin pulled him out of the stupor.

Where are you? One of the cops just told me that there's been an accident. What the hell is happening?

I'm out on the course, Von wrote back. I'll meet you inside the ballroom in a minute. Make sure you keep that news about the accident to yourself until further notice.

On the way to the terrace, Von slowed down when he heard one of Dani's officers say, "So I get that you think these incidents are all linked. But why would someone want to kill your ex? And why here, during the auction?"

"That's what we're trying to figure out. Maybe someone's attacking people I know to send the message that I'm next? And they're committing these crimes under RSP, as if they've got a vendetta against Von's company. Hell, at this point, they're occurring under the watch of Maxwell PD, too. So there are layers to these crimes that need to be peeled back. Immediately."

"I agree. Because this town is on the brink of going into full panic mode…"

The exchange sent a ripple of alarm through the cool night air. As the commotion raged on, Von's mind moved in slow motion. He couldn't grasp the reality that Maxwell was under attack yet again.

The sound of Dani's voice lifted the fog. He jolted, reminded that she had asked him to inspect the scene inside the club. But he couldn't move. It was as if his feet were planted to the course, ensnared within the tree roots twisting beneath the surface.

"Von!" she called out once more. "Please let me know what's going on as soon as you make it back inside."

There was an edge to her tone, as if she were irritated that he was still there. Her wide-eyed expression screamed *Get the hell off the fairway and do your job!*

"I'm on it," he called out, forcing his limbs to cooperate.

Right before entering the club, Von composed a message to Dani.

Please do not go home alone. Let me follow you there. I want to make sure you arrive safely.

He sent it, purposely leaving out the part where he'd be staying the night. Their hometown, which they'd believed was finally safe again, had been thrust into yet another terrifying nightmare. No matter what it took—even if he had to sleep on the porch—there was no way in hell Von would be leaving her side.

Von's phone buzzed with a response from Dani.

I'd like that, thanks. By the way, I just received word from the hospital. Jeffrey didn't make it.

Chapter Seventeen

Dani's living room had been transformed into a war room of sorts as she was surrounded by case evidence. Several weeks had passed since Jeffrey's death at Gibson's, and the Maxwell PD was no closer to identifying a suspect. So she'd called her crew over in a bid to regroup, refocus and review everything they'd collected thus far.

Troy and Chloe had taken over the couch while Dani and Von set up shop along the floor. Dani had tasked each of them with specific assignments. As she examined crime scene photos and surveillance footage, Troy combed through police reports, Chloe reviewed autopsy results, and Von analyzed cell phone records.

Plates of half-eaten chicken pad thai and crab rangoon were strewn between empty water bottles and soda cans. The television and streaming systems were off and the team was locked in—taking notes, exchanging commentary and working to building a solid criminal profile.

When her phone pinged, Dani dived for it, groaning in frustration at the sight of a CNN news alert. No calls or texts from her digital forensics investigator. She refreshed her email inbox. Nothing there, either.

"Still no word from Chuck?" Von asked.

"Nope." Dani peered at him from across the coffee table. She wasn't surprised that he knew exactly what was bothering her. Their thoughts flowed like a synchronized dance. Over a short period of time they'd become completely aligned, able to read each other's thoughts and finish each other's sentences as if they'd been lovers for a long time.

"Wow," Chloe said, her lips bending into a mischievous smirk. "It's amazing how all it took was one glance for Von to know what's going on with you, Dani."

"Well, that shouldn't come as much of a shock," Troy said. "Didn't Von pretty much admit to stalking Dani over the years?"

"I *studied* Dani over the years," he quickly clarified. "Not stalked. There's a huge difference."

"Yeah, Troy," Dani chimed in, swatting her brother's leg. "Now cut it out and get back to work. We've got a crazed killer terrorizing our town. There's no time for jokes here."

"There's always time for a little laughter. The mood is heavy enough as it is. Nothing's wrong with sprinkling in some comic relief to lighten things up."

All eyes turned to Dani when she drew a sharp breath. Just as she fixed her lips to respond, Von raised a hand in the air. "All right, all right. Like the chief said, let's get back to business. Dani, what's the latest on Jeffrey's crime scene? Any new evidence come to the forefront?"

"Well, the surveillance cameras did capture him heading out to the terrace about thirty minutes before his body was discovered. He was seen taking a pack of cigarettes out of his jacket, so I'm guessing he went out there to smoke."

"Did the footage capture anyone going outside after him?"

"Nope. Which tells me whoever did this is familiar with Gibson's layout and knew how to get out there without being seen by the cameras."

Flipping her notebook to a blank page, Chloe asked, "What

about the cameras out on the fairway? Did those capture anything?"

"They didn't. The video feed doesn't reach the eighteenth hole, where Jeffrey's body was found. And it was so dark out on the course that the footage didn't cover anything beyond the terrace."

"Okay, so..." Chloe hesitated, her eyes shifting around the room. "What did Kevin have to say for himself?"

"What do you mean?" Von asked.

Scooting toward the edge of the couch, Chloe said, "I'm referring to him disappearing around the time that Jeffrey's body was found. Did you talk to him about it? Or did you, Dani?"

The room fell silent. When Dani caught Von's eye, she read straight through to his thoughts. *I'll let you take this one, because if I do, it won't be pleasant.*

"We didn't talk to him about it," Dani told her, "but Von and I have been tracking his movements. Nothing about his behavior has been suspicious. He's been everywhere he's said he's going to be, and he isn't acting any differently than normal."

"Since we're doing some digging here," Von said, "what's up with those Maxwell PD officers who took issue with Dani after she was promoted? I believe it was Simons, Henderson and Kenin, correct? Have you all looked into those guys? Asked them any questions or monitored their movements?"

"Actually, we have," Troy countered. "Dani and I assembled a small team of officers who we trust to keep tabs on their whereabouts. We've been tracking them for weeks. So far, no one has done anything to cause suspicion."

Tapping his pen against the table, Von replied, "Yeah, well, I've been keeping a very close eye on Kevin, and like Dani said, he hasn't done anything to cause suspicion, either."

"Yet," Chloe muttered under her breath.

Von let off a sarcastic chuckle. "At one point, you all

thought *I* was your suspect, didn't you? Obviously you were wrong then. So why is it so hard to believe that you're wrong about Kevin?"

"Look, I know that man is your bestie or whatever," Chloe said. "But I'm not putting anything past anybody. We see who Maxwell's first serial killer ended up being—"

"Whoa, slow down," Von cut in. "These are two completely different situations."

"Are they really, though?"

"Guys," Dani interjected, her arms slicing through the air like a boxing referee. "Please. All this sparring back and forth isn't gonna get us anywhere. Now until we get some solid proof of suspicion, wrongdoing…*anything* that would point us in the direction of a suspect, we won't be making any more accusations. Got it?"

"Got it," the group muttered, each of them busying themselves to avoid eye contact.

After checking her email once again, Dani sensed the room's energy had turned toxic and knew she needed to shift topics. "So, I'm still waiting to find out whether Chuck was able to get something on those anonymous texts and calls. But I'm not getting my hopes up since he's come up short every time he's tried."

"But I thought he was working with some sort of new and improved software," Troy said. "That hasn't helped?"

"No. Or not yet at least. Like I've always said, whoever we're dealing with here knows exactly what they're doing. Remaining anonymous is their area of expertise. These obsessive hacker types have a way of staying ten steps ahead of law enforcement."

"True. You never know, though. Chuck is a pro himself. He doesn't usually take this long to get back to you with information, so maybe he's got something this time."

"Let's hope so." Dani picked up a magnifying glass and held it to a photo taken at Lieutenant Edwards's crime scene. The picture trembled in her hand as she homed in on his legs, twisted like crooked tree branches along the stairwell floor. His eyes were eerily wide open, as if fixated on the perpetrator who'd taken his life. His gaping mouth appeared as though it'd been calling out for help. But no one arrived in time. The terror emanating from the image was palpable. Intrusive. Personal…

Dani's throat burned as she muttered, "*Maniac.* Who the hell would do something like this? It is just pure hatred."

"Yes it is," Von agreed. "What's interesting is how each crime scene is so different. It's as if the suspect has no real modus operandi. Our first victim was shot in the head, the second was stabbed in the chest…"

"And the third was poisoned with strychnine—"

"Wait," Von interrupted. "He was? You didn't tell me that."

"I could've sworn I did. There's been so much going on that it's hard to keep up. But anyway, yes, there were traces of the drug in Jeffrey's system that came up in his toxicology report. And the medical examiner discovered a needle mark in the crook of Jeffrey's neck."

"Wow…okay. I'm not familiar with strychnine. How does it affect the body?"

"It's a white, odorless crystalline powder that can cause respiratory failure, and a lethal dose goes into effect quickly. Jeffrey's official cause of death was acute hypoxemic respiratory failure. And before you even ask, no. There wasn't any DNA evidence found on the syringe. So the killer must be using gloves when committing these crimes." Dani paused, shuffling through a stack of photos before pulling one from the scene of Brandy Orland's attack. "And while his murder was horrible, it wasn't nearly as gruesome as the others. There's no rhyme or reason to the way these victims were killed. But we all know the one thing that connects them."

When Dani pointed at herself, Von raised a finger in the air. "Yeah, I do know. All too well. I hate to sound like a broken record here, but I'd be remiss if I didn't mention the connection to RSP. My company almost lost the upcoming wine festival gig because these crimes happened on our watch. Whoever's behind this is going out of their way to destroy RPS's reputation."

"Duly noted," Dani said as frustration whirled through her chest like a tornado, poised to strike. She grabbed her phone and pounded the home screen. "Why in the hell hasn't Chuck gotten back to me yet?"

"Maybe he's still trying to figure out—" Von stopped abruptly when her computer pinged. "Wait, is that him?"

"Yes, *finally*..." Her fingers flew across the keyboard as she frantically scanned the email. Within seconds, she tossed her head back and stared up at the ceiling. "Oh my God..."

"Let me guess," Troy said. "He wasn't able to track down the owner of the cell."

"No, he wasn't. But that's not all." Spinning the laptop around, she shoved it toward Von. "You read it. I—I can't."

"Okay..." he replied pensively. "I've got an update, Chief. While I was searching for the owner of the burner phone, I fell into a bit of a rabbit hole and ended up on the dark web. I discovered something pretty unsettling on a bounty site. Someone listed all of your personal information—your full name, home address, phone numbers, email addresses, and a photo of you. They've offered a $50,000 reward to whoever can kidnap and murder you—'"

"Wait, *what*?" Chloe screeched. "Did you say kidnap and murder?"

"That's what it says," Von choked, reaching across the table and clutching Dani's hand.

Troy leaned in and gave her shoulder a supportive squeeze. "Was Chuck able to trace that back to whoever posted it?"

"Doesn't look like it. Apparently, the person said that anyone interested can email them for details and left an address. Chuck sent a message but hasn't heard back yet. He's extracting metadata in hopes of tracking the IP address back to the owner."

"I'm so sorry, Dani," Troy said. "Just know that we're all here to protect you in every way. What else can we do to make you feel safe in all this?"

"We can stick close by for starters," Von interjected, not waiting for her reply. "Which is why I really don't think it's a good idea for you to stay here alone, D."

"I second that," Chloe added.

Dani shot to her feet and stormed the kitchen, grabbing a bottle of wine. "I really hate this. I'm Maxwell's chief of police! I was trained to do this. I've got a security system in place, surveillance cameras all around the house, several weapons within reach. And yet here I am, needing to be babysat."

"This isn't about being babysat, Dani," Von responded, his low tone offsetting her hard edge. "We hate that this is happening to you, too. But unfortunately, it is. This killer is slippery. He has a way of getting around whatever safety protocols you've got in place. So we've gotta keep our eyes on you while staying two steps ahead of him—"

"But *how*?" Dani interrupted, balancing four glasses in her arms while making her way back toward the living room. "We haven't been able to pull that off so far, which is why we've got three deaths on our hands."

"By being more diligent in our pursuit," Chloe rebutted,

taking the glasses and passing them around. "As the threats escalate, additional security measures would not only help ensure your safety, but they'd also give you extra peace of mind."

"Exactly," Von cosigned. "I think it would be a good idea for us to work in rotation, along with the rest of Maxwell PD. I know you've had officers sitting outside the house, but considering what we're dealing with here, it wouldn't hurt to have someone on the inside with you as well. The three of us could alternate staying here with you, just to make sure this lunatic doesn't follow through on his word."

"Or that someone else doesn't take him up on his offer and try to collect that $50,000 bounty," Troy added.

"All right, all right," Dani surrendered, taking a series of quick breaths to stay calm. "Fine. We'll work out some sort of surveillance routine."

She could sense the collective sighs of relief filling the room. But their comfort didn't erase her underlying fear. On the surface, Dani wore a tough facade. Yet beneath it all, she valued their persistence. There was no denying that the killer had the upper hand, and she'd become his number one target. What troubled her more, though, was that despite their tireless efforts—the digging, the researching and the analyzing—they still had no viable suspect.

"Keep the faith, D," Von said, as if he were able to read her thoughts. "Trust me, we're gonna catch this psycho before he or anyone else gets to you."

When he slid around the table and wrapped her in his arms, Dani caught a glimpse of Troy's and Chloe's expressions. They looked on with wide eyes, seemingly caught off guard by the unexpected show of affection.

Dani ignored them, resting her head against Von's chest. Her breathing steadied against the beat of his heart. As the pressure of the situation mounted, the past seemed insignificant compared to the urgency of what lay ahead.

In that moment, Dani let down her guard and allowed herself to be vulnerable. To admit that she couldn't do this alone. And that she needed the help of those around her.

Chapter Eighteen

"Do you need anything else right now, Chief Miller?" the server asked.

"Another Perrier would be great, thanks."

"You got it. Be right back."

Dani watched as she walked away, then checked her phone again. Von was supposed to meet her at the Zonian almost an hour ago. He'd been held up at the office, running background checks on several new employees he'd recently hired. Von hoped that adding more officers would boost security enough to deter the killer from striking again on their watch.

Any idea when you might be here? she texted. I'm almost done with my salad and struggling to hold off on ordering a burger until you get here...

The pair had agreed that making a public appearance together would present a united front, signaling that their agencies were collaborating to bring down the killer. It was Thursday—the most popular night of the week at the Zonian. Considering how bold their suspect had been thus far, Dani figured he just might be there to indulge in the half-priced cocktails, enjoy the karaoke battle, scope out his next victim.

That wasn't the only reason she'd invited Von to hang out. Dani needed to catch him up on the afternoon's town hall meeting. They were held once a month inside City Hall's vast auditorium, and usually lasted about an hour. Since things normally ran so smoothly around Maxwell, attendance was oftentimes low.

That afternoon, however, there wasn't an empty chair in the building. Once the local government representatives, department heads and community leaders were done presenting, Mayor Cox opened up the floor for questions. And that's when all hell broke loose.

For over two hours, concerned citizens expressed their fears over the killer and questioned the Maxwell PD on what they were doing to protect the community. A few of them even made suggestions on how law enforcement could bring down the suspect. From consulting with a psychic to flooding the sky with drones to surveil every inch of the city, Dani had heard it all.

Mrs. Roswell, a lifelong citizen and self-proclaimed co-mayor of Maxwell, stood in front of the microphone reading a manifesto on how Dani should use truth serum on persons of interest and AI-powered facial recognition software to track their movements.

Her boldness prompted a slew of others to speak their minds, including Mr. Green, one of Maxwell's oldest residents. He'd teetered up to the mic on his cane while pumping a fist in the air, yelling, "Maxwell PD isn't doing anything to catch this animal. All of our lives are at risk. Either do more to keep this community safe, or I'll make a move to defund the police!"

Dani had tried her best to defend the department. Aside from offering up safety advice, she'd shared how extra patrol officers were out on the streets. Police presence was heavy at every event. A tip line had been established. The department was using advanced forensic techniques to gather evidence. And Maxwell PD had joined forces with RPS to help bring down the killer.

"Well, that simply isn't enough, now is it?" Mr. Green had rebutted before the townspeople broke into thunderous applause.

By the time the meeting ended, Dani realized there was no getting through to the community. When it came to the investigation, they weren't concerned with the department's intentions, plans or case updates. The Maxwell PD wouldn't be back in the townspeople's good graces until an arrest was made.

The buzz of her cell phone sent Dani lurching against the back of the booth.

Please calm down...

But these days, panic mode had taken over her normal disposition. Being in the middle of a crowded bar wasn't helping matters. Dani felt as though all eyes had been on her since the moment she'd sat down. It was no wonder, considering the investigation was being covered on the local news almost daily and the national news weekly. Every journalist, true crime expert, lawyer and law enforcement officer was asking the same questions. Who was terrorizing the town of Maxwell a second time around, and why hadn't the police brought the killer to justice?

The Maxwell Times had resorted to reporting on the case every single day. Oftentimes, their coverage was splashed across the front page. From "Has the Community Lost Faith in the Maxwell PD?" to "Is It Time to Bring in the Feds?," the headlines were becoming more scathing by the week.

Dani vented her frustrations on her Caesar salad, stabbing her fork into a thick clump of romaine lettuce. She was tempted to send it back and request another one with the dressing on the side. But she was too hungry to bother. She'd arrived at the police station that morning before seven o'clock, bypassing breakfast and working straight through lunch. By the time she had arrived at the Zonian, Dani was ready to order everything on the menu.

Her phone pinged again, this time with a series of texts from Von.

I am so sorry I'm running late! I ran into a glitch with these background checks.

Now the computer system just shut down…

Kevin had to leave and pick up his wife. I'm gonna have to finish this job solo. Be there soon as I can!

The server approached with Dani's drink. "Here you go. I'll come back over as soon as your guest arrives—"

"Change of plans. He doesn't know what time he'll be here. So I'll go ahead and order the turkey burger with cheddar cheese and a side of sweet potato fries."

"You got it. I'll get that order in and tell the cook to put a rush on it."

"I'd appreciate that, thanks."

Dani sipped her water while eyeing the crowd. A woman was standing on the stage, the straps on her red terry cloth halter top hanging down by her elbows as she belted out a drunken version of Alanis Morissette's "You Oughta Know." Hordes of people were waving their hands in the air while singing along with her. A few of them were huddled together, whispering while tossing skeptical side-eyes in Dani's direction.

Ignore them, she told herself as flames of irritation burned her neck. Just as she turned back to her salad, Dani's cell pinged again.

"Von," she muttered, "you'd better tell me you're on the way."

She swiped open the home screen without checking the notification. A text from an unknown number popped up.

Good evening, Chief Miller. I love that cool tan blazer you're wearing. How's your salad?

The phone fell from her hand and crashed against her plate. Gripping the edge of the table, Dani spun around and peered through the crowd. She didn't notice anyone looking back at her.

Who the hell is this, she typed, and where are you?

A reply came in within seconds.

It's me. The one you've been looking for. And I'm here, with you. At the Zonian.

Why don't you come over to my table so that we can talk face-to-face? Dani fired back.

Nah, no thanks. I'd rather do it this way. I'm actually enjoying watching you squirm in your seat while you wonder where I am. Is it frustrating, knowing that I can see you but you can't see me?

Anxiety clawed at her chest as Dani reread the message. Keeping her head down, she slowly raised her eyes and scanned the immediate area. Checked to see who was typing on their cell. That wasn't effective considering half the people there had their faces buried in their phones.

"Here you go," the server said, placing her burger on the table. "Can I get you anything else?"

"No, this is great, thanks."

The moment she walked off, Dani pushed the plate away.

Her appetite had been devoured by a chilling sense of unease. Sliding her hand toward her hip, she gripped the handle on her Glock 22, just to make sure it was still there.

Her cell lit up with another message.

What, no response? And why aren't you eating? Is something wrong with your burger?

Dani took screenshots of all the texts and forwarded them to Von.

I need for you to get to the Zonian immediately! she told him. The killer is here, and he's watching me!

As soon as she hit *Send*, Dani called Troy and told him to get there, too, then put out a blast text to all her officers.

I'm on my way! Von wrote back. I'll have as many of my guys there as I can gather...

His message was followed by a slew of other officers, confirming they were en route.

Be sure to surround the entire building, Dani replied. I'll have the manager shut this place down. No one is coming in or going out until we find our suspect.

She hit Send and sprang to her feet. Then froze.

Slow down, Dani told herself. *Respond to his text. Don't let on that you're about to take him down...*

She straightened her pants legs as if that's why she'd stood, then gradually took her seat. Grabbing the phone, she replied to the suspect.

If you must know, my burger is undercooked. So I need to send it back. In the meantime, I wish you'd stop by and say hi. But I'm not surprised you won't. We both know you're nothing but a coward...

Dani sent the text while keeping her eyes peeled to the door. When her server came into view, she discreetly called her over.

"Is something wrong with your dinner, Chief Miller?"

"Oh, no, not at all. Everything looks delicious. But I do need to speak with the manager. Would you mind sending him over?"

"No problem. I'll go and grab him now."

Dani's cell vibrated in her hand with a new message from the suspect.

What are you up to, Chief Miller? Texting nonstop, not sending the burger back after claiming it's undercooked... Are you putting together a plan to try to catch me?

As she surveyed the scene once again, sirens wailed in the distance.

"Damn it!" Dani hissed, mad that she hadn't told her officers to cut them.

A young man approached the table, sweeping his blond bangs away from his pale green eyes. "Hey, Chief Miller. I'm the manager, Bobby James. What can I do for you?"

"You're...the *manager*?" She'd never seen him before. He was all of five two and didn't look a day over fifteen.

"I am. And I already know what you're thinking. Just so you know, I'm twenty-two. I just look like a kid."

"Okay, well..." Dani paused, realizing that she hadn't thought out exactly what to say. She didn't want to alarm Bobby and cause a panic. But she needed to come up with something that would convince him to secure the place. "I, um, I was wondering if you could lock the front and back doors as soon as possible, and not let anyone in or out. I've been alerted that one of the patrons had a very expensive watch stolen, and I'm hoping to figure out who took it."

"Oh, yeah, of course. I'll lock them now. Is that your backup I hear pulling up?"

"Yes, it is. So why don't you go on and secure those doors so we can get this process started?"

He gave her a thumbs-up before rushing off. Just as she grabbed her cell to call Troy, it vibrated with his name on the screen.

"Hey!" she yelled over the music. "Are you here?"

"I am. So is the rest of the team. We've got the place surrounded."

"Good. Turn off the sirens and lights and come inside. Is Von here yet?"

"I think I see him pulling up now."

A knot of tension loosened as Dani blew a heavy sigh. "Great. Send him in, too."

She headed toward the front door. On the way there, the manager flashed her a quick military-style salute. She mouthed the words *thank you* and waited for her officers to approach. Just when she spotted Troy, her cell pinged again with another text from the unknown number.

Aww, silly rabbit, tricks are for kids, and you just got played! You really think I'm dumb enough to stick around and get caught? I've been gone, bitch. Just wanted you to know you're being watched. As usual, I'm one step ahead. You hunt down killers like an amateur. While you're reading this, I'm zooming past all your officers. Your little sting was a waste of taxpayers' dollars. See you next time, when I might actually make a move and take you out...

Dani jumped at the sight of Troy banging on the door. She opened it, her sagging expression etched in defeat.

"Don't tell me," he said.

"Yeah," she croaked, stepping outside and peering down the street. "He got away. *Again.*"

Following her toward the curb, Troy asked, "Wait, how did the suspect know that you were here tonight?"

"I don't know. But trust me, I'm gonna find out."

Chapter Nineteen

Von pulled into the Desert Grove Ranch, the crunch of gravel beneath the tires barely audible over the crowd's boisterous chatter. Maxwell's wine festival had started less than thirty minutes ago, and the parking lot was already packed.

After searching every aisle for a space, he managed to squeeze his car in between two oversize SUVs along the last row. He hopped out and hurried around to open the passenger door.

Dani was slow to exit. She didn't want to be there. She'd actually considered speaking with the Chamber of Commerce and having the festival canceled altogether. Another public event seemed too dangerous. The last thing Maxwell needed was another death on its hands. But Von had managed to talk her out of calling it off. The townspeople were already living in fear. Postponing such a huge tradition would only cause more alarm.

"Plus it'll make you look unsure of yourself," he'd insisted. "As a matter of fact, you'll appear unsure of your entire team, as if you're admitting that the Maxwell PD doesn't have things under control."

"Well, obviously we don't," Dani retorted. "We're investigating a third murder, and despite the escalating threats, the violence…we have no real evidence and suspects. This entire town thinks the Maxwell PD is a complete failure."

"Wait a sec, don't you think that's a bit of a stretch? Your department isn't new to this. You caught a killer before. And you'll do it again."

"That's the hope. Now let's see if it will become a reality. Because right now, all I know is that the fear among the community is rising. There are only so many PR statements we can release about how we're doing all we can to protect the town and solve this case. Eventually, everyone is gonna lose faith in us. A lot of them already have."

Brewing frustration stopped Dani from continuing. The daily criticism of the Maxwell PD was overwhelming enough. There was no need for her to pile on.

These days, even Chloe was being harassed. After word spread that she was the one who'd lured Maxwell's first serial killer to town, her *Preyed Upon* podcast listeners demanded that she cover the town's current murders. Chloe insisted the cases were still under investigation and there wasn't enough information available. But Dani knew the truth. Chloe was hesitant to speak on the department's failure to catch the suspect.

Forcing herself out of Von's car, Dani's stomach twisted into tiny tremors of tension. Memories of that chilling night at the Zonian still haunted her, two weeks later. Despite their best efforts, the Maxwell PD couldn't identify a suspect. Tracking the perpetrator through blurry surveillance footage inside the jam-packed, dimly lit bar had been impossible. Investigators weren't able to distinguish the perpetrator's DNA from the crowd's considering the vast number of people leaving evidence behind. And once again, the text messages that had been sent to Dani came from an untraceable number.

She did, however, figure out how the suspect had been keeping track of her whereabouts after Von discovered an AirTag tucked behind her license plate. A forensic analysis of the small circular device turned up nothing—no fingerprints and no trace evidence. Dani had no idea how long it had been there. But knowing that she was being hunted like prey left a cold, unsettling feeling in the pit of her gut, as did the realization that the killer was simply waiting on the perfect moment to attack.

The one thing she did have on her side this time around was the support of RPS. While Dani and Von had been leaning on each other more than ever, their dueling agencies just recently put an official end to their feud. The decision was driven by the killer's shared vendetta against both Dani and Von, prompting the Maxwell PD and RPS to team up for the wine festival in hopes of preventing another tragedy.

There was, however, one caveat—Kevin. Von was still convinced that he had nothing to do with the crimes. After he'd disappeared right before Jeffrey's death at Gibson's, Dani wasn't so sure. Uncertainty led her to ask Troy and Chloe to keep constant watch on him during the festival.

"You all right?" Von asked as they headed toward the entrance.

"I'm fine," she lied, unwilling to admit that her nerves were buzzing like a colony of frenzied bees. "I guess I'm not in the mood to be under everyone's microscope today. All the scrutiny, the judging… I just wanna do my job and catch this maniac."

"Just stay the course, Chief. You got this."

While his words were reassuring, they did little to dispel the chilling uncertainty looming in the air.

Deep breaths, Dani told herself. *Head up, shoulders back...*

As they approached the sprawling ranch's heavy wrought iron gate, she was hit with the rich aroma of wine mixed with the earthy scent of damp soil. Her darting eyes settled on the pastel haze stretched across the sky. The low-hanging afternoon sun cast a warm golden glow over rows of wine-tasting booths.

Attendees sauntered from one wooden booth to the next, sipping from their glasses while nibbling on a variety of cheeses. Their colorful, breezy attire was a stark contrast to Dani and Von's dark slacks and crisp button-down shirts. As the event's festive energy rippled through the crowd, it left Dani longing for things to be different. For there to be no criminal terrorizing their town.

"Looks like the organizers got a big turnout," Von said. "Which means we've got our work cut out for us."

"Yes, we do. So let's stay vigilant and keep our focus sharp."

"Absolutely." He hesitated, his words trailing off as he glanced around the sprawling event area. "You know, for some reason, I can't imagine the killer would be bold enough to try to pull something off today, knowing we're on high alert."

"I can. Remember the criminal profile we came up with that night with Chloe and Troy? The suspect loves sensationalism. And craves attention. He's a sociopath who gets a thrill every time he commits a murder. That excitement intensifies when he gets away with it. I believe he'll continue to chase that high until he can't anymore."

"Meaning when he gets caught?" Von asked.

"Exactly. But for today, I've got a plan. Our killer may very well be out here somewhere, hiding in plain sight. So I'll be zeroing in on each guest, hoping that something speaks to me." Dani pivoted, sweeping her arm across the rustic landscape. "So, what are you thinking? Should we split up and take a look around, see what we see, then reconvene a little later?"

"Why would we do that? Are you afraid to be seen with me?" Von's lips curved into an uneven smirk. But his blunt tone was unmistakably serious.

"Of course not. I just figured we'd cover more ground faster if we separate."

"I'd prefer that we stick together. You never know what we might run into out here."

"Okay then. Let's get moving."

As the pair set off toward South Holland Winery's booth, all eyes were on them. Most people spoke, but their greetings were chillier than normal. Dani wasn't surprised, nor did she bother mentioning it to Von. It was to be expected. The mood in town had been anything but upbeat in recent weeks. Being surrounded by so many familiar faces in one place only amplified the weight of the Maxwell PD's failures.

Dani cast the cold reception aside and plastered a pleasant expression on her face while moving through the crowd. Her instincts were piqued as she studied each passerby and took in every conversation. She was aware that their suspect knew how to blend in. So she searched for something deeper. Signs of someone whose behavior was slightly odd. A person who was overly fidgety, with jerking eye movements or uncontrolled bodily gestures. So far, no one was sticking out.

"I'm glad to see that all of our officers are positioned at their respective posts," Von said. "But have you noticed the strange looks people are throwing at us?"

"I have. And I don't know if it's because they're surprised to see us together, or upset that I've yet to solve this case. Either way, I'm being cordial all while ignoring it. My focus is on making an arrest. Not winning a popularity contest. Last year the town hated me until the suspect was apprehended. Then all of a sudden I was the queen of Maxwell. Their words, *not* mine."

"Yeah, I assumed that."

"My point is I don't expect this go-round to be any different than the last. So let's just block out the noise and stick to the mission at hand."

"You got it, Chief."

Von rolled up his sleeves as the sun blazed overhead. Dani stepped back, letting him take the lead as she observed him effortlessly engage with the attendees. His presence was commanding yet approachable. Authoritative yet charming. There was an air of confidence with each conversation that drew people in, including Dani. She'd spent so much time resenting him that she hadn't realized how well-liked he was within the community.

While Dani had left the romance that sparked between them simmering in the background, she couldn't ignore the stream of emotions stirring within her. She was left questioning whether she'd made the right decision, putting him on hold while allowing the investigation to consume her.

Deep down, she knew she had. There would be plenty of time to explore their connection once the case was solved. Or so she hoped…

But Dani's concerns didn't end there. She was still struggling with the idea of publicly dating Von. He'd chalked it up to her reluctance in telling her father, and he wasn't completely wrong. She had no idea where her dad stood these days when it came to the Reed family, and she wasn't eager to find out for fear of his response. Dani knew she'd have to share the news with him eventually—but it would be on her own terms, in her own time.

"I know the day is still young," Von said. "But so far, nothing is sticking out. I'm not seeing any strange faces or behaviors, no weird incidents…"

"Yeah, same. But like you said, it's early. Anything could happen. There's still plenty of time for things to go left."

"True…" Von shoved his hands inside his pockets and spun

a full circle. "I've been meaning to ask about the list of vendors and staff members working the event. Were you able to get a hold of it?"

"I was." Dani pulled out her cell and forwarded him the list. "I just texted it to you. We can check that against all the booths, and each of the staff members are required to wear badges. So if we see people lurking in the background, or walking around unauthorized areas, they should be wearing a lanyard."

"Cool. I'll be sure to keep an eye out for that."

Dani's phone buzzed with a text from Troy.

Chloe and I are here and we've got eyes on Kevin. He's been chatting with a few vineyard owners near the north side of the ranch. We're being discreet, but we're on it.

Good, Dani wrote back. Thanks for the update. While you're at it, keep a close watch on our guys, too. If anything starts to look suspicious, alert me immediately.

"Everything all right?" Von asked.

The question startled her, almost rattling the phone from her hand. "Everything's fine," she blurted, shoving the cell in her back pocket. She searched Von's curious expression, wondering if he'd seen the text. Dani hadn't told him that Kevin was being watched by her team and certainly didn't want him to find out that way.

An obnoxious burst of laughter drew their attention to a group huddled nearby. Dani's instincts flared. Something about their exaggerated movements seemed off.

"Do you recognize any of those people standing near the Starlit Cellar's booth?" Von asked.

"I do. I think I've seen a few of them around Cole's. And… wait, isn't that Lieutenant Edwards's wife, Camille?"

"Judging by the pictures I've seen of her when I was looking through their social media accounts, I believe so. Ironically, I saw that she's connected to my father on LinkedIn, so I guess they know each other. Any idea who the man is holding her hand?"

Dani's eyes snapped down to their intertwined fingers. "Ooh, I didn't even notice that. I don't know, but he looks familiar." She pulled out her phone, opened Facebook and scrolled to the lieutenant's personal page. "Yep, just what I thought."

"What's that?"

"His name is Reginald Duvall. He's the president of the ski club that Lieutenant Edwards belonged to."

"That's…interesting."

"Very interesting." When Dani noticed Camille's eyes narrow in her direction, she subtly angled herself away. "Her husband's barely been gone for three months and here she is, cozying up to one of his closest friends. On a side note, Camille was never too fond of me. I think she took issue with the fact that Lieutenant Edwards and I grew close once he became my mentor. She always gave me the cold shoulder whenever we saw each other."

"Humph… So, if we're talking possible suspects, then it sounds to me like Camille could be in the running for a couple of reasons. One, she may have wanted to kill her husband to pursue a relationship with his friend. Two, if she's holding a grudge over her husband's role in helping you become police chief, then having another killer on the loose would be the ultimate revenge. Does that make sense, or am I reaching?"

"No, that makes perfect sense. And at this point, nothing is a reach. Especially since I saw her at the mayor's fundraising event *and* the art auction. Back when we first began investigating the lieutenant's murder, was our focus on the wrong family member? Should we have been more concerned with the wife rather than the son?"

"Maybe," Von said. "But I thought Camille had a solid alibi on the day Lieutenant Edwards was killed."

"She had a friend corroborate her whereabouts. But maybe I need to obtain more solid proof of that. Also, I should add that Reginald was at Cole's the day of the murder. Every member of the lieutenant's ski club was there."

"Ooh…and the plot thickens. What do you think? Should go over and say hello?"

"Good idea. I'll let you take the lead since she'll probably be more receptive to you than me."

The instant they reached the group, Camille yanked her hand from Reginald's grasp.

"Ch-Chief Miller," she stammered, her jovial expression bending into awkward surprise. "I—I'm surprised to see you here at the wine festival."

"Why? I always attend this event."

Waving a bony hand in the air, she tossed her head back and forced a giggle. "Oh right, right. I guess I was thinking you would be on duty, manning the station rather than indulging in alcoholic beverages."

She pressed her pointy elbow against Reginald's chest, prompting him to join in on the feigned laughter.

"Well, you're right about a couple of things," Dani responded, taken aback by the couple's matching neon white veneers. "I am on duty, which is why you don't see me drinking any alcohol. And I'm deep into the investigation, which is why I'm out here with my squad, patrolling the event rather than manning the police station."

Dani waited on her to inquire about the case since she hadn't once called in to the department for an update. Instead, Camille turned to Von and puckered her artificially inflated lips.

"Hello, Mr. Reed Jr. Are my eyes deceiving me, or has RPS landed on good terms with the Maxwell PD?"

"Hello, Mrs. Edwards. No, your eyes are not deceiving you. My team and I have joined forces with the police department to assist in the investigation. Chief Miller and I couldn't allow some rivalry to compromise public safety. So here we are. Doing all that we can to solve the case. Also, you have my condolences. I've heard nothing but wonderful things about your husband. Losing him has obviously been a huge blow to the entire community. How are you and your family holding up?"

Camille sucked in her jaws, as if the question had soured inside her mouth. "We're, um…we're holding up the best we can. The support of friends has been tremendous. I don't know if I could've gotten through this without them."

Yeah, I bet, Dani thought, watching Camille recoil beneath her steely gaze. Reginald's feet shuffled to the side, as if he were attempting to create distance between himself and the group.

A staff member from a nearby booth approached, offering wine samples. Camille took two and downed them both within seconds. While she made a feeble attempt at small talk by asking Von about his father, Dani's phone pinged. It was a text from Chloe.

Slight new development. We overheard Kevin talking to a couple of RPS officers. He mentioned Von hanging up photos of the victims in his office, just to keep the cases at the forefront of mind. Kevin begged him to take them down because he hated seeing their faces every day. I thought that was odd and worth mentioning… Nothing suspicious with Maxwell PD, though.

Good to know. Von and I have what could be a major new lead that we didn't see coming. Meet me by the information booth in thirty minutes and I'll tell you all about it.

Chapter Twenty

Von's eyelids fluttered before gradually opening. He let off a deep yawn followed by a full stretch, awakening from the best sleep he'd had in weeks.

The corners of his lips curled into a satisfied smile at the sight of Dani's bare shoulders peeking over the soft gray sheets. He resisted the urge to slide over and kiss her neck, massage her awake and indulge in another round of love-making.

Their night together certainly hadn't gone as expected. From the moment they'd arrived at the wine festival to the moment they left, the pair had been on edge—cautious, mindful and keeping a watchful eye throughout. By the time the event was over, exhaustion weighed heavily on them both. But so did an overwhelming sense of relief as things ended without incident.

On the way home, their hunger pangs superseded the fatigue. They ended up grabbing dinner and drinks at the Copper Plate. Afterward, when Dani invited Von in for a nightcap, he couldn't say no. One thing led to another, and they ended up in bed together.

Von was hoping that Dani wouldn't jump up the second her alarm went off and kick him out. Nothing would make him happier than holding her in his arms a little longer and making love to her once again.

Bzzz...

Dani's vibrating cell sent her stirring. Von moved in closer as she arched her back, her breasts spilling out from underneath the sheet.

"Good morning," she murmured, her eyes barely open when she reached for her phone.

"Morning..." His muffled voice vibrated against her skin as his lips caressed her shoulder. "How'd you sleep?"

"Really well. Better than I have in weeks."

Pulled her toward him, he whispered, "I'm assuming that's because I was here with you?"

"Maybe so. I'm sure all the kisses and touches you showered me with until I couldn't hold my eyes open helped, too."

"And just think, there are so many more where those came from..."

She pushed her body further into his embrace while checking her phone. "Chloe's asking if I want to meet up for coffee before I go into the station."

"What are you gonna tell her?"

"That I'll have to catch up with her later."

"Good answer," Von said, gently nuzzling her ear.

Dani typed a quick reply, then set her phone back on the nightstand. Taking that as a cue to proceed, Von glided his body between her thighs. His arousal pressed against her, hardening when she drew him deeper. Her hands cradled his face. Pulled him into a kiss that began as a slow burn, their tongues tangling in a sensual dance. A rough, throaty moan hummed in the back of Von's throat when her hips rose to meet his. Just as their bodies began moving in perfect sync, Dani's phone buzzed again.

"Damn it," Von grunted, collapsing onto his back.

"Now I *just* told Chloe that I'm in the middle of something."

"Oh? You actually told her that I'm here?"

Dani's silence was all the answer he needed—she hadn't.

"Never mind," he muttered, rolling over onto his side.

"Come on, Von. It's not like that. I—I'll tell her later. I haven't been keeping you a secret."

"I'm really not a secret, though, am I? With the exception of last night, we haven't been seeing each other romantically. So technically, you have nothing to hide."

Dani remained quiet, her expression solemn as she reached for her phone again. Her refusal to communicate pushed Von to want to say more. To admit that his feelings for her hadn't changed. If anything, they'd deepened.

Just let it go, he told himself, clenching his jaw to keep quiet. She still seemed conflicted about her feelings for him. And he refused to put himself in a vulnerable position again, just to be rejected.

Dani moved toward him, the warmth of her hand resting against his chest easing his nerves. As their fingers intertwined, Von struggled to resist pulling her in again and returning to the moment they'd shared before Chloe's interruption.

The brief taste of what she'd given him weeks ago—a glimpse of the life they could share—left Von wanting more. But when Dani cut him off without warning, both his heart and ego were left bruised. Then last night, she'd revived him, quenching a thirst he'd been desperate to satisfy. Von hoped it wasn't just a brief reconnection, and that this time, she'd stay by his side.

He glanced over and noticed that her phone screen was black. "What's going on with your cell?"

"It's dead. I was so preoccupied when we came to bed that I forgot to plug it in. So I don't know if that notification was another text from Chloe or a call that I missed."

"Just let it charge for a few minutes. It'll get some juice

and you'll be able to tell. In the meantime, where did we leave off?"

"Right here, I believe..."

Dani slowly repositioned herself, her body curving over Von's. She straddled his hips. Took all of him in her hand while sliding down his chest. Just as she disappeared beneath the sheets, her phone rang.

"Ignore it," he insisted, shivering beneath the brush of her lips. "Just keep going."

"You know I can't do that." She crawled back up, reached for the phone, then jolted upright.

"What's wrong?"

"I've got a ton of missed called from several of my officers. Even Natalia called from the station. This is not good." Dani's fingers stumbled over the screen as she struggled to dial out. "*Troy*," she snapped, putting the call on speaker, "what's going on?"

"You need to get to Desert Grove Ranch right now! A woman's body was pulled from the reservoir this morning."

DANI'S HEART STUTTERED wildly as she and Von rushed to the water's edge. Officers and the medical examiner were already on the scene, hovering over the victim.

"Chief," Troy said, his expression eclipsed by a cloud of dread, "the medical examiner confirmed that the victim has no vital signs."

Pulling a sharp breath, Dani nodded, the musty scent of damp earth stirring a pang of nausea. She swallowed hard and approached the body. There was something hauntingly familiar about the woman. The way her dark, shoulder-length hair clung to the sides of her heart-shaped face. Her petite figure, on full display underneath the muddy lavender maxi dress clinging to her limbs. Those wide-set hazel eyes, half opened and lifeless, holding on to what she'd seen during her final moments.

"Is it just me," Dani said, the words tightening in her throat, "or do I look eerily similar to this woman?"

Von and Troy glanced at each other, neither of them quick to speak up.

"So it's not just me."

"I, um…" Von mumbled, "I didn't want to say anything, but yes, she does look like you."

"Yeah, I noticed it, too," Troy added.

"Do we have an ID on her?" Dani asked.

"Not yet. But no one here recognizes her. We're thinking she might be from out of town and here for the wine festival."

While crime scene investigators snapped photos with digital cameras, Dani fumbled for her cell, her fingers quivering as she took pictures of her own. "Who found her?"

"Two ranch workers," Troy said. "They were checking the water troughs when they came across her body."

Kneeling beside the victim, Dani studied her, wincing at the shock throbbing in her head. The resemblance between them was uncanny. It was as if someone had pulled Dani's reflection from a mirror and discarded it there.

"Somebody did this to scare me," she choked. "There's no question that all these murders have been personal. But this one? This crosses the line."

Von crouched down beside her and turned to Troy. "Did anyone notice trauma to her body when she was pulled from the water? Or could this have been an accident? I'm thinking that she may have drunk too much and fallen into the reservoir."

The hope in his voice was unmistakable. Dani couldn't help but appreciate his optimism. But there was no denying that this was a targeted attack. The killer's actions were far too methodical, and there was a twisted method to his madness. He'd intentionally murdered Dani's doppelgänger, fully aware that she would detect the resemblance. This wasn't just a crime. It was a message. And she'd heard it loud and clear.

Pointing toward the victim's throat, Troy added, "We did discover several red marks along the back of her neck. We're thinking that if this was a homicide, those may be the result of an attacker holding her head underwater."

Dani stood, her feet unsteady as she shook with a sudden surge of panic. "This is unreal. Four deaths in less than four months, and not a suspect in sight. No real evidence. Nothing. I've been racking my brain nonstop trying to figure out the motive behind these crimes. Is it some random local, enamored by all the attention the last killer got, so they're thirsty for a little notoriety? Is it someone who's related to the last killer, who might be out to avenge his arrest?"

"Those are all valid theories," Von said. "And let's not forget the one we came up with yesterday connected to the lieutenant's wife, her new boyfriend..."

"Let's not overlook the Maxwell PD and RPS officers who're still holding on to unresolved issues from the past," Troy chimed in. "One thing we do know for sure is that whoever it is, they know what they're doing. I'm still thinking they've got some sort of background in criminal justice."

"You're right. But that doesn't bring us any closer to identifying a person of interest," Dani countered, her gaze drifting as she turned away from the victim. "If anything, it only broadens our search. So let's think about it. We've got another death on our hands that's connected to an event that RPS was hired to work, and the Maxwell PD was patrolling. But this time around, none of us know this victim, correct?"

"Correct," Von and Troy replied in unison.

"However, this is our first victim that we're thinking isn't from Maxwell. And she just so happens to resemble me. To a T."

"Which could just be a coincidence," Von suggested.

"I highly doubt that. Our killer doesn't seem to be doing anything just for the sake of it. Every murder has been calculated. A direct hit that's targeted the two of us." Dani pointed at her brother without talking her eyes off of Von. "Troy, could you please excuse us?"

Without waiting for a reply, she grabbed Von's arm and pulled him away.

"What's the problem?" he asked, his head pivoting in confusion. "Did I say something wrong?"

"No, you didn't. But I've got a question for you that I need to ask in private. And I want an honest answer. Did you tell Kevin about us?"

Von grimaced, his expression contorting into a mix of shock and frustration. "*Wow.* That was the last thing I was expecting you to ask. What does that have to do with—"

"Could you please just answer the question? Does Kevin know about us?"

"Yes. He does. Now, why are you asking me that in the middle of a crime scene?"

"Von, think about it. Kevin can't stand me. He's *never* liked me. That man has despised me since we were kids, and it's all because of you. And because of your father's hatred toward my family. He's followed up behind you like a little lapdog for as long as I can remember—"

"Dani," he interrupted. "Kevin is my closest friend and business partner. Not my lapdog."

"Correction. Kevin is your employee. Not your business partner. There's a huge difference."

"Look, I see where you're going with this, and you're wrong. Kevin's not your guy. He isn't a psychopath. He did not commit these crimes to retaliate against the Maxwell PD or RPS. And he certainly didn't do it to get back at me because of my relationship with you."

"What about the victims' photos you had hanging up in your office?"

"What about them? And…wait." Von paused, running his hands down the sides of his face. "How do you even know about that?"

"Don't worry about it. Just explain to me why Kevin begged you to take them down, *knowing* they were inspiring you to help solve this case."

"First of all, he didn't beg me to do anything. Kevin mentioned that seeing the victims' faces made him a little uncomfortable. But that's because they serve as a constant reminder that we've got a deranged assassin running around town. *Not* because he's the one who killed them."

Moving in closer, Dani jabbed a finger toward Von's chest, her fiery glare burning with intensity. "Listen to me. I wanna know where Kevin was last night. I want a list of everything he did, from the time he left the wine festival to the time of our victim's death. Can you get that information for me, or do I need to bring him in for questioning?"

"I'll get it for you. And honestly, you don't have a valid reason to bring him in, other than your unsubstantiated suspicions. If you do, it really wouldn't been a good look. We just settled our differences with the Maxwell PD. After experiencing so much dissension, our agencies are finally on good terms. We're working together to solve this case. Please don't ruin that over some baseless personal issues."

"Baseless personal issues?" Dani retorted, flinching in disbelief. "I'd like to think that my reasoning behind his possible motives are logical and well thought out. But I hear what you're saying. And since our agencies are finally on good

terms, I'll fall back and let you gather that information for me. In the meantime, I'll also be speaking with the owner of the ranch and the workers who found the body, and collecting the surveillance footage from last night. If I can get some solid proof of who's behind this attack, then we won't have to worry about my unsubstantiated suspicions."

Von lifted his hands in the air, as if to surrender. "I hope you're not taking what I said personally. Like you, I'm trying to get to the bottom of all this and make sure we remain on good terms in the process. I'd just suggest that you don't lose sight of the other possible suspects we're investigating."

"Trust me, I won't lose sight of a thing. I am a professional. I'm not just focusing on your friend. Now if you'll excuse me, I need to jump in with my team. I'll catch up with you later."

Von's chest rose, as if he were about to make a statement. But Dani walked off before he could speak. She was done with the conversation. Arguing in circles wasn't going to solve a thing. Collecting evidence would.

She checked in with the medical examiner, who was busy running a swab underneath the victim's fingernails. After confirming that the victim was deceased, she called Troy over.

"I'm going to touch base with the ranch's staff and look into getting the CCTV footage. I'll meet you back out here and see what you've discovered. Any luck so far?"

"Not yet. But we're still searching. Hopefully something will turn up soon."

"All right. Keep me posted."

Dani marched toward the main lodge, ignoring the look of distress on Von's face as she walked by. She hated the fact that they'd spent such an intimate evening together, enjoying each other's company after thinking they had finally gotten a break from the case.

The pleasure, however, was short-lived. They quickly found

themselves back at a crime scene, succumbing to the pressure of another murder. Conflicts flared between them, and as they grew more at odds with each other, it felt like they were no closer to capturing the killer.

Dani's determined stride slowed when her cell phone buzzed. She expected it to be Chloe, frantic for an update. But a text from an unknown number appeared.

Her heart hammered against her rib cage as she opened it. The phone almost slipped from her hand at the sight of a photo. It was an image of the victim who'd just been pulled from the reservoir. Another message soon followed.

Oops! I did it again. I committed another murder, thinking I'd killed YOU. Little did I know I murdered the wrong person! Oh well... But the good news is I'm getting closer to the right one. Chief Miller, count your days, bitch. You're definitely next...

Chapter Twenty-One

Von trudged alongside Dani as they made their way down Willowbrook Nature Reserve's sandy walking path. The sun was barely up before she'd dragged him out of bed, insisting she needed to hit the trail and release some anxious energy.

The idea hadn't sat too well with him. Von had envisioned the pair sleeping in, then spending a lazy Sunday morning filled with hot coffee, an Uber Eats breakfast delivery, and a movie or two, then diving back into the investigation later in the day. But he'd agreed to Dani's suggestion, hoping the sun's warmth and the sweet, earthy scents carried by the breeze would be enough to soothe her frazzled nerves.

A week had passed since the wine festival, and the case continued to dominate their every waking moment. The number of theories they'd brainstormed and leads they had dissected were endless. The pair managed to move past their disagreement at the latest crime scene after she'd received the threatening text. That jolt of reality was a harsh reminder that they needed each other now more than ever, regardless of their differences. A fractured partnership between them would give the killer the upper hand, distracting them from their number one goal—capturing him.

Dani and Von had reexamined every crime scene that week, hoping to discover overlooked evidence. They hadn't. They'd watched endless surveillance video footage once again. Questioned Cole's Ski Resort members. Called up a number of people who'd attended the mayor's charity event, the art auction and the wine festival, hoping someone would recollect something they'd seen or heard that could help the case. Once again, they hit a dead end.

The pair visited the crime lab to follow up on evidence collected at Desert Grove Ranch, but the results came back inconclusive. The medical examiner ruled the victim's cause of death as homicide by drowning. Her name was Stephanie Hunter, and she had in fact been visiting from Phoenix for the wine festival. As the text to Dani had suggested, it was a case of mistaken identity, and Dani was the intended target.

When she'd brought Lieutenant Edwards's wife in for questioning again, Camille insisted that she had been at a book club meeting during the afternoon of his death. To prove her innocence, the club's president showed police Ring camera footage from her home on the day of the meeting. Camille's entry and exit times confirmed she was not at Cole's when her husband was murdered.

Camille's boyfriend, Reginald, had left the resort late that morning to visit his mother at the Chandler Creek Nursing Home. Investigators followed up with the front desk clerk, who confirmed signing Reginald in at 11:21. That was well before the time of the crime.

During their interrogations, Dani pushed harder, zeroing in on their suspicious behavior at the wine festival. Both Camille and Reginald cracked under the pressure, admitting they were embarrassed that Dani had caught them together so soon after Lieutenant Edwards's murder. Admittedly, they'd turned to each other for support, which led to something more. What started as a simple need for comfort spiraled into a whirlwind romance—one they hadn't planned but couldn't seem to stop.

"We've got to do something big, Von," Dani said, her shrill

voice shaking him from his thoughts. "Something risky and unexpected. Something that'll catch the killer off guard and get him on our turf."

Von peered at her while she readjusted her bright yellow leggings, mesmerized by the curve in her hips. He tried to keep his eyes on her face and focus on her words. But he couldn't resist admiring how her spandex workout attire clung to her alluring silhouette.

Instead of suggesting they turn around and go back to bed, Von asked, "What did you have in mind?"

"I don't know," she huffed rapidly, her words keeping pace with her racing feet. "Maybe we could set up some sort of sting operation, you know? Something on a grand scale, since the killer clearly likes to pull stunts at large events. We could put on a music festival featuring local artists, or a town picnic, or maybe a parade..."

Von stared up at the brilliant blue desert sky, as if the answer was hidden within the scattered clouds. He watched them drift aimlessly. Listened to the crisp dry grass and rustling leaves of shrubs. Took in the vast open flatland's muted palette of browns and tans, dotted with scattered cacti. It all brought on a calming sense of peace. He suddenly understood Dani's need to spend the morning there. It was the perfect place to think. To get grounded. And come up with a new plan of action.

After several moments of contemplation, Von slid an arm around her waist and led her toward a small wooden bench tucked beneath a paloverde tree. Its slender, twisted green limbs provided a fragrant umbrella of shade.

"Let's sit down for a minute," he said. "And talk this through. Because I think I've got an idea. RPS's twenty-fifth anniversary is coming up soon. What if we throw a party celebrating that? We could do something at the Blanche Hotel. Something fancy that would garner a good amount of press."

Dani's back straightened against the palm of his hand. "That's a good idea. A great idea, actually. You know what would be even better?"

"What's that?"

"If Maxwell PD teams up with RPS and we throw the event together. You know, just to reinforce the fact that our agencies are on good terms and working together to solve this case. I could even host it, if that's something you'd be interested in me to do."

"Of course I would. I'd be honored. Plus that would be the perfect setup for the killer. He'd go down in history if he pulled off another murder during an event of that magnitude."

"Thing is," Dani said, "we're not gonna let that happen. We'll have so many officers in place and ready to strike that it *couldn't* happen..." Her voice drifted as she picked at a chip in the wood. "But here's my question. Since both of our fathers would want to be there, how do you think they'd feel coming face-to-face with each other?"

"Honestly, considering how much time has passed, I think they'd be willing to put their differences aside. At least for one night. Don't you?"

"I do. How awesome would it be if they ended their feud altogether? Who knows, maybe our display of unity would force them to realize that it's gone on for entirely too long. I mean, seriously, at this point, do they even remember why they're mad at each other?"

"Ha!" Von chuckled. "Probably not. Maybe if they see the positive exchanges between our agencies in person, that'll help mend things."

"That, and the fact that they'll pick up on all the good energy and chemistry between us, too."

Von sank back, his eyes locked on Dani. "Hold on, are you saying what I think you're saying?"

"What, that I'm ready to go public with our relationship?"

He nodded, unable to formulate an actual response.

"I think I am."

"Dani..." Von sprang to his feet and lifted her in the air, twirling her around. "I know we're talking about a murder investigation here, and this is not the time to celebrate. But in the middle of all this madness, hearing you say that made me one happy man."

"Good," she replied, her voice muffled as it vibrated against his neck. "I know how much it means to you, so, it's time for me to get past my issues and start living for myself." She took a breath, her gaze meeting his. "I've been thinking a lot lately, about how much I've let fear control me. Fear of what people will think, what my family will say… Hell, even what strangers might think. I've been living for everyone else but myself, and I can't do that anymore."

"Can I just say that I love where your head's at?"

"Yeah, me, too. It's time for me to stop hiding. Stop worrying about everybody else's opinions, including my father's. If I keep letting that fear hold me back, I'll never live for me. And that's what I want. For the both of us. So, what's next? Should we start planning this event? Toss out some dates, make calls, take notes, coming up with an agenda?"

"Oh, trust me. We're going to do all of the above. But for now, let's just take a moment to celebrate the fact that I came up with such a brilliant idea, shall we?"

"You are so full of yourself," Dani said, her hands sliding across his shoulders. Just as their lips met, her phone buzzed.

"Can we *please* just have a peaceful morning for once!" Von exclaimed.

"It's probably Chloe. I'm supposed to help her brainstorm new ideas for her upcoming podcast episode."

"Good," he murmured in between kisses. "That doesn't sound too pressing. Which means you can save it for later."

"Now would you treat Kevin that way?"

"In this exact moment? Yes, I would."

"That just means I'm a better friend than you," Dani quipped, pulling her cell from her cropped yoga jacket. "See, I'm glad I checked. It isn't Chloe. It's Chuck. Maybe he's emailing me with an update."

"Okay, well, for Chuck, I'll back off."

Dani scanned the message, her smiling shriveling into a rigid line.

"Uh-oh," Von said. "I don't like that look. What does his message say?"

Shoving the phone toward his chest, she said, "Here. Why don't you read it for yourself," then turned away, refusing to look at him when he grabbed it.

"What's with the sudden cold should—"

"Just read the damn message, Von!"

"All right, all right! I will…"

Chief Miller, I've got an update for you. And it's pretty shocking to say the least. I was able trace that bounty post that I discovered on the dark web back to an email address. It's Info@ReedProtectiveServices.com. So looks like someone from Von's company may be behind this. I'm still working to connect the email to an IP address. I'll keep you posted on my progress, but that's what I've got for now.

Von dropped the phone down by his side and reached for Dani. "Babe, come on. I know you're not falling for this. I mean, do you actually believe that one of my officers would be behind all this? After all the surveilling I've done, and—"

"Just stop it," Dani interrupted, snatching the phone from his hand. "Stop trying to explain your way out of every single thing. I've suspected that Kevin was involved in this for quite some time, yet you kept trying to talk me down, insisting that I was wrong. Because he's your friend. He's your employee. He's so *loyal*."

"And my opinion of him hasn't changed. I still believe all those things to be true. What I cannot believe is that we're going through this again. And that you're actually falling for it! Our suspect has been after us both for months. Imagine how he felt when we finally put up a united front. He's obviously trying to tear us apart by hacking into my company's network, or…or spoofing RPS's domain name. I don't know. But please tell me you can see through these fraudulent tactics as clearly as I can."

"All I see is that your company's name is connected to a threat against me. So, no. You and I are not on the same page. At all. But things will become crystal clear once Chuck gets me that IP address. Although I've got a hunch that it's gonna fall right back on your so-called friend, Kev—"

Before Dani could finish, Von brushed past her and headed down the trail. "You're wrong, Chief Miller. And this time, once you realize that, I don't know if I'll still be here for you."

Chapter Twenty-Two

RPS's anniversary gala was in full swing. Von glanced around the Blanche Hotel's elegant Aurelia Grand Ballroom, impressed with its transformation into a silver-and-white wonderland. Crystal chandeliers shone a soft glow over exquisite floral arrangements. A red carpet stretched across the entryway, where a professional photographer captured guests as they arrived. The tables were covered in rich satin linens, adorned with silver candelabra-style lamps and flickering votives. And the room was filled with attendees draped in dazzling evening gowns and impeccably tailored tuxedos.

As far as Von was concerned, Dani was the most beautiful of them all. He wasn't used to seeing her so made up. It looked as if she'd stepped straight off a runway in her strapless chartreuse floor-length gown. Its daring, high-cut slit rose up her leg, baring a flirtatious glimpse of skin. The keyhole cutout revealed a seductive peek of cleavage. Her hair, which had been pulled into a smooth, high crown bun, put her ethereal makeup, dangling crystal earrings and slender neck on full display.

A few weeks had passed since their fallout over the RPS email address incident. Determined to clear his company's name, Von had commissioned Chuck to conduct a comprehensive forensic analysis of every RPS employee's electronic devices. Vindication came with the conclusive findings—

none of the staff members' network identifiers matched the data extracted from the bounty post.

Dani's skepticism, however, lingered. "Who's to say one of your guys didn't use an outside device?" she'd probed.

Von decided not to press the issue. The only way to truly convince Dani would be to catch the killer. Nevertheless, Chuck's findings had eased the tension between them. And the facts still remained true. They were stronger together and couldn't afford to be torn apart. They still had a deadly predator to catch.

So far, tonight's celebration had gone off without a hitch. Von almost forgot the real reason they were there. Both he and Dani remained on high alert during the first hour, making sure that the Maxwell PD's surveillance room was properly set up inside the hotel's presidential suite. Snipers were positioned around the building, poised and ready to act if necessary.

But as the evening wore on, Von's guard slowly began to slip. The joyous energy buzzing throughout the ballroom, the congratulatory greetings from guests and the warm camaraderie felt at odds with the unnerving possibility that their killer might be among them.

The thrill of the night occurred when Von's and Dani's fathers exchanged cordial greetings with each other. They'd later sat at a table together, sipping cocktails and sharing a few laughs over filet mignon. Von couldn't help but wonder if his connection with Dani had brought on the unexpected truce.

And now, as he watched the two men chatting amicably, Von felt a sense of satisfaction. Even if the killer wasn't captured that night, the settled beef would be well worth the effort.

When the band launched into a soulful rendition of Bobby Caldwell's "What You Won't Do for Love," Von strolled over to the bar and asked Dani to dance. He caught a subtle wink of approval from Chloe before escorting Dani onto the dance floor.

As they swayed to the music, Von's gaze drifted over the crowd before returning to her radiant face. He couldn't help but notice the glimmer in her eyes. It was a spark that he'd missed seeing over the past few weeks.

"You look stunning tonight," he told her. "I just had to get that in. And now that I have, I'll focus on the task at hand. Have you checked in with your team inside the surveillance room?"

"First of all, thank you. Secondly, yes I have. They said everything looks to be running smoothly. So far, no signs of suspicious activity."

"Good. But let's not allow that to go to our heads. Stay vigilant. Unlike the wine festival, our suspect may not wait until this event is over to make a move. We do know he's comfortable here at the hotel since he got away with murder once before. So at this point, anything is possible."

"Trust me, my eyes are wide open. We're all on full alert. On another note, can you believe that our fathers are actually sitting together, chatting each other up and toasting to RPS's anniversary?"

Von's lips spread into a satisfied smile as he glanced over at their table. "No, I absolutely cannot. Who would've ever seen this day coming?"

"Not me, that's for sure. For them or for us."

Sliding his finger underneath her chin, he raised Dani's head until their eyes met. "I've got a question."

"I'm listening…"

"I know that we're just getting back on track after the whole RPS email debacle. But I want to revisit the conversation we had about us moving forward together as a couple. Out in the open. If that's something you're still interested in, do you finally feel comfortable telling your father about us? Tonight? Especially now that he and my father seem to have squashed their beef?"

"I do," Dani murmured, cupping his face in her hands. "But considering how all eyes are on us right now, we might not even have to. Whatever we decide, let's wait until the time is right and the coast is clear. I don't want to lose focus and allow talk of *us* to overshadow why we're here tonight. Does that make sense?"

"Yes, that makes perfect sense," Von said, drawing her closer as their bodies continued moving to the music. "I'm just glad that we're finally on the same page."

"Same. Because at one point, we weren't even in the same book."

"Ha! Facts…"

As the music slowly faded, Dani's father took center stage.

"Good evening, everyone!" he roared into the mic. "If I may interrupt for a brief moment, I'd like to say a few words."

"What is that man doing?" Dani whispered. "This was not a part of the agenda…"

"Yeah, well, neither was a reconciliation between him and my dad. So maybe he's been moved to get up there and say a few words. I'd say this is a good thing. So let's just go with it."

"Agreed. Not that we seem to have much of a choice," she said as her father continued.

"First of all, for those of you who don't know me, I'm Gene Miller, Maxwell's former chief of police."

The crowd burst into a round of cheers and whistles.

"Thank you, thank you. Now, for those of you who *do* know me, I'm sure you're well aware of the history between the Maxwell PD and the founder of RPS, Mr. Hamilton Reed. If you don't, long story short, Hamilton and I *hated* each other. For years!"

When everyone broke into raucous laughter, Gene held a hand in the air to quiet them. "Hamilton was my biggest rival, my biggest competition, and here's something he may not know, my biggest inspiration. After tonight, I think it's safe to say that I've got my old friend back. Hamilton, I'd like to congratulate both you and your son, Von, who just so happens to be standing in the middle of the dance floor with my daughter, Chief Danielle Miller..."

"Oh, no he didn't," Dani moaned as all eyes turned to them.

"Ohh, but he did," Von uttered through a toothy grin. "Just smile and nod."

"Sorry to put you two on the spot!" her father interject. "But anyway, like I was saying. Hamilton, Von, congratulations on Reed Protective Services' anniversary. You built an amazing business from scratch, and despite our issues, I've always admired that. So, job well done, and here's to continued success."

"Hear, hear!" Hamilton shouted, leaping from his chair and thanking Gene with a big bear hug. As the men raised their glasses for a toast, the band launched into an up-tempo rendition of Louis Armstrong's "What A Wonderful World."

"Wow..." Von said, tightening his hold on Dani's waist. "I never would've seen that coming. For an impromptu speech, it was pretty fantastic."

"Yes it was," she replied, dabbing the corners of her eyes. "I didn't see it coming, either. If it weren't for some crazed killer terrorizing our town, I'd say that tonight has been pretty damn perfect."

"And I'd concur."

"Chief Miller?" Von heard someone chirp through his earpiece. "Come in, Chief Miller."

Her smile shriveled into a downward curve as she dipped her chin. "Chief Miller here," she announced discreetly into a tiny microphone taped inside her dress's bustline. "What's going on?"

"Chief, this is Officer Rose. We wanted to check in and let you know that everything still looks to be secure. No suspicious activity. The officers guarding the exterior haven't detected anything peculiar, either."

"Good, thanks for letting me know. We've got a couple more hours to go before the event is set to end, so let's stay alert. Keep your eyes open. You already know what we're dealing with, and tonight would be the perfect opportunity to pull off a sensational stunt yet. So stay sharp."

"Will do, Chief. We're on it."

"Ten-four," Dani said before taking Von's hand in hers. "It's good to hear that all is well."

"It certainly is. But like you said, we've still got a couple more hours to go. So we'll see if we get through the rest of the night without incident. And with that being said…" He held their clasped hands in the air. "What's up with the public display of affection? You sure you're ready for all that?"

She leaned in, her lips gently melting into his. "Yes, I am. Especially since I'm the one who made the move. Now, may I interest you in glass of fresh berry spritzer since we're not allowed to drink while we're on duty?"

"Yes, you may. Thank you."

Heads turned as they set off toward the bar hand in hand. While the whispers were low, the stunned expressions spoke volumes, loud enough for anyone to grasp.

"Do you see all the attention we're getting?" Von asked, his tone tinged with amusement despite hoping Dani wouldn't let the chatter get to her.

"I do. And I'm ignoring it. Consider tonight our soft launch."

"I think I like the sound of that." Von took his glass from

the bartender and held it in the air. "A toast. To us. May we continue on this path, and ride it as far as it'll take us. No matter where it's going, long as I'm with you, I'm good."

"Cheers to that."

The clink of their glasses was drowned out by the blare of a fire alarm. Within seconds, the water sprinkler system activated.

The ballroom spiraled into hysteria. Guests ran for cover while hotel employees scattered in search of the fire. Pulling off his jacket, Von tossed it over Dani's head and led her to a side entryway.

"This is it!" he yelled, squeezing his eyes shut as water drowned out his vision. "The killer is on the move!"

"And so are we!" Pulling her gun from her black leather garter belt, Dani jumped into action. "You know the plan. Touch base with RPS and make sure your officers are in place. My team should already be in motion. I'll take the back stairwell and check in with my officers in the surveillance room. Keep your phone close. We'll circle back in ten minutes."

"Got it! Oh, and hey, Dani?"

"Yes?"

"Be careful, and… I love you."

She clung to his arm, her fluttering eyelids suddenly growing still. "Stay safe. And I love you, too."

Chapter Twenty-Three

Dani's heart pounded against her rib cage like a frenzied bird struggling to escape its cage. She hit the stairwell and climbed the stairs two at a time. Sharp cramps shot through her calves from the strain of her pewter pumps. She gritted her teeth, pushing through the pain as she made her way to the third floor.

Bursting through the door, she tore down the hallway, her heels snagging on the plush blue carpet. The fibers almost yanked them off her feet while she sprinted toward the room.

Dani fought to control her erratic breathing as the pounding in her head grew louder. The rush of terror mixed with fierce determination clouded her mind, eclipsing all hope of calm. This was it. The killer had struck. Her chance to take him down before he took her out had finally arrived.

She threw open the door. Rushed over to the dining room table where her officers had set up shop. They weren't there.

Dani spun a three-sixty. The room was completely empty.

"Officer Rose?" she called out.

No answer.

"Officer Shields?"

Still no response.

"*Anybody...* Where are you?"

She dashed through the living room. Checked the bedroom, then both bathrooms. They were all empty.

"What in the..."

Pulling out her phone, Dani called each officer who'd been operating the room. No answer.

She ran to the computers and frantically scanned the monitors. Black-and-white feeds from various areas around the hotel flashed across split screens. Dani peered at the lobby. The officers weren't there. She checked the common spaces, elevators banks and stairwells. No sightings there, either.

Dani switched to the feed inside the ballroom. The entire area was consumed by wall-to-wall commotion as guests skidded across the slick parquet floors. Elegant updos were reduced to drenched, matted messes, while smeared makeup accentuated the horror etched on faces. Elaborate attire was soaked, clinging to shivering bodies. Amid the havoc, Von and his officers, along with the Maxwell PD, fought to usher attendees toward the mezzanine. Yet among the frenzy, there was still no sign of her surveillance team.

"This is Chief Miller," she barked into her mic. "Can somebody from the Maxwell PD please come in?"

"Chief, this is Officer Mixon. I'm still out back, patrolling the parking lot. Several of our guys were called inside the ballroom by Officer Miller after the fire alarm went off."

"I've lost contact with the majority of the team, and the surveillance room is empty. Has anyone seen Rose and Shields?"

"I have. They came out here and checked in before heading back inside to help get the crowd under control."

"Wait," Dani said, her voice rising over the sirens wailing in the distance, "why did they leave the suite? I need at least one officer keeping an eye on things at all times."

"According to Rose, a member of the hotel's staff came up and told them that you requested their assistance inside the ballroom."

Dani's knees went limp as a flash of heat swelled in her gut.

Steadying herself against the table, she iterated, "A hotel staff member? The only employee who knew we were inside this suite is the manager. And he wasn't instructed to do anything. Did you get a physical description of the staffer?"

"I did not. And I've lost contact with most of our officers, too. I don't think they can hear us over all the noise."

Spinning around in a panic, Dani surveyed the room, her eyes darting to ensure she was alone. "Listen, I'm heading back down to the ballroom now. What's the word around the premises? Do guests seem to think this whole alarm thing is suspicious, or that there's an actual fire somewhere in the hotel?"

"Honestly, Chief, I'm hearing a little bit of everything. But considering we've got a killer on the loose, most people are thinking there's more to it than just a fire."

"Got it. Thanks for the insight. I'll check back in with you soon."

On the way to the door, Dani dialed Von's number. The call went straight to voicemail.

"Von, it's me. Apparently, the hotel manager told my surveillance team they were needed inside the ballroom. I don't know where that order came from, but something is definitely off here. I'm on my way to the ballroom back down now. See you soon."

Dani disconnected the call. Walked past the emerald-green couch. Just as she reached the hallway, the suite went dark. She whipped around and stared into a black abyss.

Get out! that inner voice screamed inside her head.

Dani lunged for the door. The second her hand hit the handle, something was thrown over her head. Wrapped around her entire body.

"Stop!" she screamed, struggling to swing and kick her way out of the tight fabric. "What the hell are you doing?"

No response. Instead, Dani was knocked to the floor. Her nails clawed at the material as she fought to free herself. But every limb was constricted, wound like a vise, rendering her almost immobile.

"Let me *go*!" Dani shouted right before a raspy voice growled, "Shut up!"

Dani's body strained against the fabric. She attempted to lift her legs. Punch her fists. Anything to break loose. Nothing was working.

Wrapped up like a mummy, she was dragged across the room. The vicious tugging tore at her skin, igniting a scorching blaze of friction burns. Dani was being flung around like a rag doll, her limbs hitting floor lamps, furniture, police equipment and whatever else was in the assaulter's path.

"Please, *stop*!" she cried out angrily.

Dread coursed through her veins as the fabric clung to Dani's skin. Salty droplets of sweat stung her eyes, intensifying her confusion. The ability to breathe was stifled by her stuttering heartbeat. The dense air grew heavy with heat as the room seemed to be closing in. Every desperate move Dani made only wound the fabric tighter, trapping her in an oppressive shell of fear.

Keep trying. Keep moving!

Dani writhed her body in hopes of hooking on to something. While contorting with more urgency, she heard the attacker's breathing become increasingly strained.

I'm wearing him down...

"Ugh!" Dani grunted when her torso hit what felt like a doorframe.

Boom!

Suddenly, the sheet loosened. Dani kicked her way out. Felt around for her gun. It was gone.

Jumping to her feet, she searched for the suspect. When

a faint bit of light flashed through the room, she noticed a dark figure hovering against the window, his body parting the curtain.

"Stand down!" Dani screamed.

"Or what?" he yelled through a distorted voice.

Dani stood with her fists clenched, prepared to fight for her life. Hoping that she wouldn't go down with a stab wound to the chest or a bullet to the head—despite standing there alone in the dark with no weapon, no backup and no way to contact Von.

I cannot die tonight, she thought before yelling, "Come on! Let's *go*!"

Footsteps pounded the floor as her assailant lunged at her. Dani couldn't make out a weapon. Only two fists. She went in for an uppercut.

Bam!

A kick to the stomach sent Dani doubling over. Excruciating pain shot straight through to her back. The attacker, dressed in a black-and-white hotel uniform, hovered over her.

"Chief Danielle Miller!" he screeched in a sinister high-pitched voice. "Who the hell do you think you—"

Dani cut him off with a blow to the right jaw that landed with a sickening crack. The impact sent him stumbling backward as he gagged on a mouthful of blood. Dani kept going, unleashing a flurry of blows that released the fear and anger she'd been carrying for months. Every murder, every attack, every threat… They'd all led up to this moment. Her assailant's groans of pain were music to her ears.

A left hook to the nose sent his head snapping sideways. A right cross dropped him to his knees. The final blow, a kick to the face, sent him crashing to the floor, where he lay motionless.

"Get up!" Dani roared.

He edged toward the love seat, his legs tangling in his boots while he struggled to stand. Following after him, Dani tripped on the sheet she'd been wrapped in. She snatched it up and shook it out in search of her gun. It wasn't there.

Crack!

The room grew even darker. Dani rocked backward, her vision distorted in the obscurity of the unfamiliar surroundings. Just as it began to clear, she caught sight of a brass lamp swinging in the assailant's hands. It came crashing down toward her head. With a quick twist, she ducked to the right, narrowly missing it by inches.

Dani dropped to the floor, the carpet's rough fibers scraping against her palms as she frantically looked for her gun. Loud rumblings from behind sent her twirling around, her leg extended in a powerful kick. Dani's stiletto sank deep into the suspect's chest, eliciting a guttural wheeze.

Her attacker collapsed, then rolled over onto his stomach. Instead of crying out in pain, he was giggling uncontrollably.

Dani paused. Listened closely. The tone was shrill and squeaky. And unmistakably feminine.

"Finally!" a woman grunted. "I got to you. The one who always thought she was better than everybody else, just because her daddy was chief of police. The one who constantly bragged about following in his footsteps. Welp, you made it, Dani. But, news flash! You're a complete failure. You barely caught Maxwell's first serial killer. If it weren't for your brother and his little girlfriend, that never would've happened. This time, you're dealing with a pro. Four murders under my belt and you *still* couldn't catch me. Two attacks, countless threats, and you never did track me down. See, Maxwell PD was right. You didn't deserve that promotion. Lucky for you, nepotism!"

Dani's chest constricted, imploding under the gravity of the woman's words. That voice. So familiar, yet forgotten, until now. Her presence. Bold, obnoxious, sucking the air right out of the room…

Slamming her hand against the wall, Dani fumbled desperately for the light switch. Her eyes widened when the shadowy figure struggled to her feet, then hobbled back and forth in a fit of rage, ranting as if she were reading from a venomous manifesto.

"But look at you now, *Dani*. Even with Von's help, you still couldn't track me down! And you know what? You never will. Because you're about to die. I cannot wait to wrap my hands around your throat and rob you of your last breath. But before I do that, I just need to know why the hell you thought you could take over Maxwell. This is *my* town, bitch! Always has been and always will be. You thought you'd snatched my crown with all that attention you got from catching a killer. Ha! Now the only attention you'll be getting is the news of your death."

"You are out of your *mind*!" Dani screamed right before the woman came charging at her. She stood in a fighter's stance, fists in the air. But her badly beaten attacker was barely hanging on. A swift elbow to the left temple sent her crashing to the floor.

Darting toward the nearest lamp, Dani jabbed at the switch. The room lit up. She spun around. Stared down at the woman who'd been terrorizing her for months.

There, holding her head in agony, was Von's ex, Carmen Pendleton.

"Carmen!" she choked, stumbling against the back of the couch at the sight of her former classmate. Her petite figure was swallowed by the oversize black suit, and her hair looked to be buried underneath a short brunette wig. "*You're* the one who's been behind all this?"

Dani stood in frozen shock, waiting on her to respond. But

she didn't. Carmen's eyes were pinned to the floor. Following her gaze, Dani spotted a glint of shiny black metal beneath the love seat.

My Glock!

The women dived for it at the same time. Dani beat her there, grabbing the gun, and pointed it directly at her chest.

"Stand down!" she said right before Carmen lurched in her direction. "I swear, if you make one more move, I will shoot you!"

Carmen staggered to a halt. But her tirade continued. "To answer your question, Dani, yes. I'm the one who's been making your life miserable, just to prove your inadequacy. And I am proud to say that my mission has been accomplished."

"This is about Von, too, is it?"

"Of course it is! Because how could you actually try to take him from me?"

"*Take* him from you? You two weren't even dating!"

"If that's what he told you, then he lied. We were on a break, idiot. And then you came along with the whole damsel in distress act. *Ooh, Von, somebody's trying to kill me. Let's be friends!* I still can't believe he fell for it. Had it not been for you, he would've come back to me a long time ago. But..." Carmen's head fell as her eyes welled up with tears. Seconds later, she glanced up, her distressed expression transforming into a wicked grin. "That's why I had to teach his ass a lesson, too. Sabotage his work gigs. Prove that he's just as incompetent as you."

Carmen crept forward, her eerie gait resembling that of a predator, closing in on its prey. "You two deserve each other—"

"Listen to me!" Dani yelled, her finger tightening on the trigger. "Either back up or get shot. Your choice."

"Yeah, right. Girl, you don't have the guts to shoot me."

"But I do!" Von charged inside the room with his gun drawn. "Now follow Chief Miller's orders and stand down!" He turned to Dani, whispering, "I got your voicemail. When you didn't show up inside the ballroom, I knew something was wrong." Tossing her a pair of handcuffs, he said, "Chief, do your thing."

Dani closed in on Carmen. It was a fight to cuff her as she thrashed about in a last-ditch effort to break free. Dani and Von's combined strength quickly overpowered her resistance. He pinned down her ankles while Dani seized her wrists. Carmen's struggle intensified, but slowly, her energy waned. Once defeat set in, she finally surrendered.

Dani exhaled sharply at the sound of the cuffs clicking shut. As Carmen's head drooped, her spiked wig slipped off, exposing a stocking cap that concealed a slicked-back bun.

"All I ever wanted was *you*," Carmen spat in Von's direction. "I did everything I could to destroy anyone who stood between us. I even put that fifty-thousand dollar bounty on Dani's head, hoping I'd finally get rid of her. But you *still* chose her. Why? Look at her! Why would you want that spoiled, entitled—"

"Hey!" Von snapped. "That's enough. Chief, should I call for backup?"

"Sounds like they're already on the way," Dani replied as heavy footsteps echoed through the corridor.

Tightening her hold on Carmen's arm, Dani said, "Carmen Pendleton, you're under arrest for the murders of Gordon Edwards, Brandy Orland, Jeffrey Simmons and Stephanie Hunter. And for the threats, attacks and attempted murder against me, Chief Danielle Miller."

Chapter Twenty-Four

"Wait, so let me get this straight," Chloe said, stepping onto Dani's backyard deck. "You mean to tell me that Carmen confessed to being the killer, *while* she was attacking you?"

"Yes. That is exactly what I'm telling you. Her plan was to reveal the twisted motive, kill me, then flee the scene, just as she always had."

"Little did she know you'd live to tell your story."

"Yes, I did. My team did a great job erasing every trace of that bounty threat from the dark web, too."

Dani took a breath, her fingers trembling while pouring ice into a cooler. Recounting the night of the attack still had an emotional effect on her. It hadn't been a full two weeks since the incident. The haunting memory dredged up everything leading to that terrifying moment. The threats, the murders, the bounty on her head. Dani didn't know if she'd ever get past it all.

You will. Baby steps. Just focus on today...

At the last minute, Dani had decided to throw a barbecue for the Maxwell PD and RPS as a thank-you for all their hard work. The purpose of the gathering was twofold as they were also celebrating Troy's promotion to detective.

Dani scanned the portable buffet table, rearranging platters of corn on the cob, shrimp cocktail and Italian pasta salad to make room for Chloe's three-tier cupcake stand.

The rich, savory scent of steak filled the air as Troy manned the grill.

Guests were slowly trickling in. Everything was going smoothly—except that the men of the hour, Gene Miller and Hamilton Reed, had yet to arrive.

"Troy," Dani whispered, "are you sure Dad confirmed that he'd be here?"

"Yes. I'm positive."

"And he knows that Von's father will be here, too?"

"I didn't mention it to him, but I'm guessing he does know since RPS is being acknowledged, too."

Von slipped past Dani and set a tray of marinated rib eye steaks, lobster tails and chicken breasts next to the grill. "Everything is gonna be fine, D. I'm sure that both of our fathers will be here."

"You're right. I'm being paranoid. I just want everything to be perfect."

She surveyed the yard, her eyes lingering on each face while her hands fidgeted restlessly. Even with Carmen behind bars, Dani was still on edge. The constant urge to glance over her shoulder, double-check the car before getting in, keep her Glock within reach…those instincts hadn't faded.

"Babe?" Von whispered, giving her back a soft caress. "Everything all right?"

"Yes, it's just—I'm still a little anxious, that's all. And I hope we get a good turnout this afternoon. I want the day to go smoothly. I owe that to Troy, and to both of our agencies, to show them how grateful I am."

"Trust me, we all know that. And it's going to be a great day. So why don't you take a deep breath, relax and enjoy the party? The hard work is done. Carmen is locked up. While you're busy thanking and celebrating everybody else, it's time for you to relish that win. Now, since you like to indulge in a little dessert before the main course, how about I grab you one of those red velvet cupcakes?"

"Thank you, baby, but I'll wait," Dani murmured, brushing his lips with a soft peck. "I'm looking forward to that steak and lobster. But I appreciate all that you said. I needed to hear it."

"That's what I'm here for. Be right back. I'm gonna see if Troy needs help on the grill."

As soon as he walked off, Chloe swooped in.

"Here," she said, slipping a red plastic cup in Dani's hand. "I think you need to have a little wine. I can tell you're stressing out. But I'm glad Von's pep talk helped."

"It did. He could sense my anxiety. I honestly think all this tension stems from me blaming myself for not figuring out Carmen was the killer sooner."

"How could you, though? She managed not to leave any evidence behind. Plus she's the last person any of us would've suspected."

Dani's voice lowered as she pulled Chloe toward the side of the house. "There were definitely signs that I'd overlooked. The fact that her father worked for RPS and hated my dad because of the rivalry with Maxwell PD. That animosity trickled right down to me. Then there was the whole jealousy thing. Carmen resented all the attention I got after we arrested the first serial killer. In her delusional mind, she thought I was stealing her limelight."

"Makes sense. Carmen always did think she ran this town. But Maxwell wasn't enough for her, hence the move to LA. She never did land that A-list movie role though, did she?"

"Nope. Which is why she came running back home. Now here's an interesting side note. Carmen landed a small part in a low-budget thriller, where she played a murderous hacker. I watched it after her arrest, and so much of that film mimicked this case. That's where she learned the ins and outs of untraceable burner phones, fake email addresses and AirTags. She also knew to use public Wi-Fi to hide her IP address and wear discreet protective gear while committing the crimes. Between that and her father's knowledge of the criminal justice system, Carmen knew exactly what she was doing."

Chloe stood motionless, staring straight ahead while clutching the sides of her face. "What a psychopath. Didn't she try to launch some channel on YouTube after her acting career failed, thinking she'd become a big influencer?"

"Yep, right after she moved back home. It was called *Beauty Gets You Everywhere*. That didn't take off, either. She had about twenty-five subscribers. So she never was able to reclaim her it-girl status here in Maxwell. That's probably what really made her snap. As you know, nothing drives a narcissist to the brink of psychosis faster than the lack of attention."

"Facts. And what about Von? Were you able to prove that the crimes were aimed at him, too?"

"I was. Carmen admitted to it. She was pissed when he and I got close and took it out on us both. Her goal was to ruin RPS's reputation and put them out of business. You know, when I took her statement, she actually seemed to enjoy sharing details on how she'd gotten away with the crimes. I found out that she had been temping for an event staffing service. So she worked catering gigs at Cole's, the Blanche Hotel, Gibson's Country Club *and* Desert Grove Ranch."

"Oh, so she was already familiar with the layouts and knew how to get around the buildings."

"Exactly."

Chloe's eyes shifted away from Dani as she fidgeted with the drawstring on her army-green jumpsuit. "Hey, I've got a question. Did you ever apologize to Von for accusing Kevin of being your suspect?"

"I did. On behalf of you and me both, actually. And he graciously accepted the apology."

"Good. And *thank* you. Because I was right there with you, thinking that man was guilty. But anyway, back to Carmen. Please tell me that she's being held without bond."

"She is. And since I've got her full confession on record, she'll likely spend the rest of her life behind bars."

A loud buzz rippled through the backyard. Dani followed the crowd's gaze. A huge grin spread across her face when her father walked through the gate. Von's dad entered right behind him. The moment their feet hit the lawn, they were surrounded by guests, receiving warm hugs and cold bottles of beer.

"They're here!" Dani said to Von after rejoining him on the deck.

"Just like I knew they would be."

He leaned in and held her close, drawing plenty of raised brows from those standing nearby. Even a few low whistles blew through the breezy afternoon air.

Dani caught sight of her father raising a beer in their direction, just as Mr. Reed tossed them a thumbs-up.

"Could you ever have imagined our dads giving this relationship the green light?" Dani asked.

"Maybe not in the past. But there's no way I would've let anything stop us from being together. We'd have figured out a way to win them over."

The pair paused when Troy waved a pair of red grill gloves in the air. "Hey, everyone! The food will be done in about ten minutes. Why don't you all start lining up near the deck, and prepare yourselves for a delicious celebratory feast. While you do that, I'm going to pass the invisible mic over to one of our hosts, Von Reed, as he has a few words he'd like to say."

"Oh, you do?" Dani asked. "That's news to me." When she stepped to the side to give him the floor, he grabbed her hand and led her toward the middle of the deck. "What are you doing?"

"You'll see," Von told her, popping the collar on his blue shirt, then raising his cup in the air.

Dani, who wasn't a fan of spontaneity or surprises, shifted her weight while pulling at the frayed hem of her denim skirt.

What is he doing? she mouthed to Troy and Chloe.

They shrugged in unison, their shining eyes seemingly concealing a secret.

"First off," Von said to the crowd, "thanks so much for coming out today. To the Maxwell PD, as well as my RPS officers, it goes without saying that we are deeply grateful for your support in this latest criminal investigation. As we all know, Carmen Pendleton would still be on the run if it weren't for our fearless leader, Chief Miller."

Von paused as their guests broke into applause. When they quieted down, he took her hand and brought her closer. "Chief, once again, you have demonstrated extraordinary courage in protecting the people of Maxwell. While we honor the lives of those we've lost, it's important to remember that things could have been so much worse. But thanks to your efforts, they weren't. Your leadership made all the difference."

Holding her hand to her chest, Dani replied, "Thank you so much for that. But this was a team effort. And I know that came as a surprise to most, including me, given the conflict between our two agencies. However, not only did we join forces, but we also buried the hatchet, which brought our families together. I think I speak for us both when I say I'm extremely proud of that."

A thunderous roar boomed through across the lawn, followed by laughter when their fathers each took a bow.

"What's even better," Von added, "is that our hard work led to something more. Much more."

Dani held her breath as he handed Troy his cup, then reached inside his pocket.

"Danielle Miller," Von continued, "it's no secret that I have loved you for years. But I hid those feelings for obvious reasons. Now, *finally*, I am so glad that I can love you out in the open, and tell everyone here how much I care about you."

"I love you, too," she whispered, her heart thumping to the beat of his every word.

"There are so many things I could say to convey how excited I am for our future. However, I'll start here. Thank you for letting me in, and for allowing me the opportunity to show you who I really am."

Swallowing the knot of emotion in her throat, Dani rasped, "Thank you for looking past my feistiness and seeing me for who *I* really am."

The crowd's murmurs turned to stunned silence when Von dropped to one knee.

"Dani," he said, pulling a black velvet box from his pocket, "I never would've imagined I'd one day land the girl of my dreams. Yet here I am. And there's no place I'd rather be." He opened the lid, revealing a sparkling princess-cut engagement ring. "Danielle Sabrina Miller, would you do me the honor of being my wife?"

"Yes," she breathed, looking on blissfully as he slid the ring onto her finger.

The crowd erupted into cheers as Troy popped open a bottle of champagne.

"Congratulations!" he exclaimed, pulling his sister into a tight hug before whispering, "Make some time for me next week."

"Why?"

"Not to steal your thunder or anything, but I want you to go ring shopping with me."

"Aww, baby bro! Of course I will. And I won't say a word to our girl…"

Returning to Von's embrace, Dani raised her left hand, beaming as the diamond shimmered against their guests' cheering faces. Finally, all the torment leading up to this moment began to fade, replaced by the love of a man who'd been the one all along.

* * * * *